VINEYARDS OF HOPE

E.R. BLACKWOOD

Made with ♥ on the Notion Press Platform
www.notionpress.com

To my beloved family, first audience of this tale,

and Amay, our newborn joy, life's freshest trail.

Contents

Inspired by the extraordinary courage of
Jeannette Guyot, French Resistance heroine,
this novel pays homage to the unsung heroes
who risked everything for freedom.

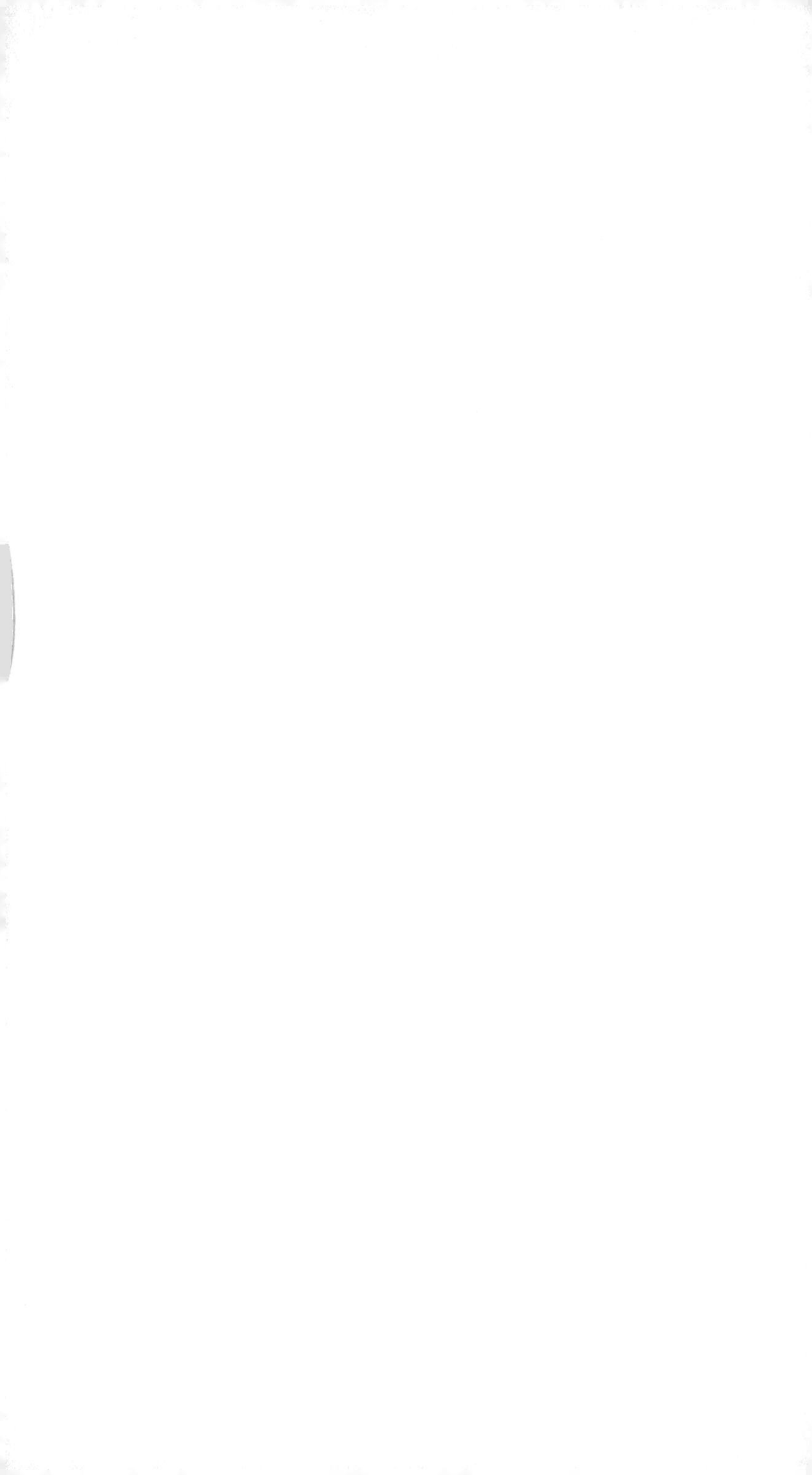

The autumn of 1940 painted the French countryside in hues of gold and crimson, but for Eduard Dupont, the world had lost its color. He stood at the window of his study in Château Espérance, watching as German soldiers patrolled the grounds of his ancestral home. The tramp of their boots on gravel seemed to mock the very name of his estate. Espérance. Hope. It felt like a bitter joke now.

"Papa?"

Eduard turned to see his daughter, Marianne, standing in the doorway. At twenty-two, she was the spitting image of her mother – all fire and determination, with a stubbornness that both infuriated and filled him with pride.

"What is it, ma chérie?" he asked, forcing a smile he didn't feel.

Marianne stepped into the room, her eyes darting to the window and the soldiers beyond. "Herr Sturmbannführer Richter is here. He... he wants to speak with you."

Eduard felt his heart constrict. Klaus Richter. Once, he had welcomed the young German student into his home, had even entertained notions of him as a potential son-in-law. Now, the very thought of him in an SS uniform made Eduard's blood run cold.

"Very well," he sighed. "Show him in."

As Marianne left to fetch their unwelcome guest, Eduard moved to his desk. From a hidden compartment, he withdrew a small notebook and a fountain pen. With quick, practiced strokes, he jotted down a series of numbers and letters – troop movements, supply routes, snippets of overheard conversations. To the untrained eye, it looked like nothing more than agricultural records. But to the right people, it was invaluable intelligence.

He had just replaced the notebook when Klaus entered, resplendent in his black SS uniform. The young man – for he was still young, despite the hardness in his eyes – clicked his heels together and offered a stiff bow.

"Herr Dupont," he said, his French impeccable as always. "Thank you for seeing me on such short notice."

Eduard nodded coolly. "Sturmbannführer. To what do we owe the pleasure?"

Klaus's eyes flickered to the window, to the vineyards beyond. "I'm afraid I have some... difficult news. Orders have come down from high command. We are to requisition a portion of your estate for military use."

Eduard felt his hands clench into fists beneath the desk. "I see," he said, fighting to keep his voice steady. "And how much of my land do you intend to steal?"

A flash of something – regret? shame? – crossed Klaus's face. "Eduard, please. You must understand, I'm trying to help. If I don't do this, someone else will. Someone who won't care about preserving what can be preserved."

"Help?" Eduard couldn't keep the bitterness from his voice. "Is that what you call this occupation? This theft of our land, our freedom?"

Klaus stepped closer, lowering his voice. "Listen to me. Things are happening, changes coming that will affect all of Europe. I can't explain everything, but I can offer you a chance. A way to protect what matters most."

Eduard studied the young man's face, searching for any sign of the idealistic student he had once known. "And what would this 'chance' entail?"

"Cooperation," Klaus said simply. "Information. Your position, your connections – they could be invaluable. In return, I can ensure the safety of your family, your estate."

For a long moment, Eduard said nothing. His mind raced, weighing options, calculating risks. Then, with a heavy sigh, he nodded. "Very well, Sturmbannführer. You shall have your cooperation."

As Klaus left, seemingly satisfied with their arrangement, Eduard slumped into his chair. The weight of what he had just agreed to pressed down on him like a physical force. Collaboration. The very word tasted like ash in his mouth.

But even as despair threatened to overwhelm him, a spark of defiance flickered to life in his heart. They might take his land, might force him to smile and nod at their requests, but they would never truly own him. Never own France.

With renewed purpose, Eduard reached for his hidden notebook once more. The information he had gathered today would soon find its way to London, to the free French forces rallying around de Gaulle. It wasn't much, perhaps, but it was a start. A seed of resistance, planted in the fertile soil of oppression.

ᛈᛈᛈ

Time passed, and the war ground on. In the spring of 1942, Marianne found herself in a small café in Paris, nursing a cup of bitter ersatz coffee. Her eyes constantly scanned the room, noting each patron, each whispered conversation. In occupied Paris, paranoia wasn't just prudent – it was essential for survival.

A man entered, nondescript in a way that immediately drew Marianne's attention. He ordered a coffee, then made his way to her table.

"Mademoiselle," he said politely. "May I join you?"

Marianne nodded, her hand casually dropping to her purse where a small pistol lay hidden. "Of course, monsieur. Please."

The man sat, his movements careful, controlled. When he spoke, his voice was barely above a whisper. "The grapes in Bordeaux are particularly sweet this year."

Marianne felt a jolt of recognition at the code phrase. "But the harvest in Champagne promises to be bitter," she replied.

The man relaxed fractionally. "I'm glad to make your acquaintance, Nightingale. I bring news that may interest you."

Marianne leaned in, all pretense of casual conversation abandoned. "What is it?"

"The Americans have entered the war, as you know. But there's more. They've formed a new agency for intelligence and special operations. The OSS – Office of Strategic Services."

Marianne's mind raced with the implications. "And what does this mean for us?"

"In time, they'll be sending operatives into the field. Men and women trained in espionage, sabotage, and coordination with resistance movements like ours. When they come, your role will be crucial. Your father's... position... makes you ideally placed to gather the kind of intelligence they'll need."

Marianne nodded, pushing down the familiar surge of guilt at the mention of her father's apparent collaboration. If only these people knew the truth, knew the risks Eduard took every day to feed information to the Allies.

"I understand," she said. "I'll be ready when the time comes."

The man stood, leaving a few francs on the table for his untouched coffee. "Good luck, Nightingale. And remember – in this world of shadows, trust is a luxury we can rarely afford. Even when our American friends arrive, vigilance must be our watchword."

As he walked away, Marianne sat back, her mind whirling. American operatives. A new phase in their shadow war against the occupation. And she would be at the center of it all, whenever it came to pass.

For a moment, she allowed herself to feel the full weight of fear and uncertainty that she usually kept carefully locked away. She was twenty-four years old, for God's sake. She should be thinking about love, about building a career, about all the normal things young women her age concerned themselves with.

Instead, she was here, in this café, plotting acts of espionage and resistance that could get her killed a dozen times over. If she was caught, it wouldn't just be her life on the line. Her father, their entire network of informants and resistance fighters – all would be at risk.

But then, unbidden, a memory surfaced. Her mother, in those final days before the cancer took her, gripping Marianne's hand with surprising strength.

"Remember, ma chérie," she had said, her voice weak but filled with conviction. "In times of darkness, we must be the light. No matter the cost, no matter the danger, we must stand for what is right."

Marianne straightened, feeling her resolve harden once more. Yes, she was afraid. Yes, the road ahead was fraught with peril. But she was a Dupont, and Duponts did not shrink from duty.

ppp

Across the Atlantic, in a nondescript office building in Washington D.C., Jacob Heller sat across from a stern-faced man in an immaculate suit.

"Mr. Heller, what I'm about to tell you is classified at the highest levels," the man began. "President Roosevelt has signed an executive order establishing a new agency: the Office of Strategic Services. We're here to coordinate intelligence activities behind enemy lines. And we want you to be part of it."

Jacob leaned forward, his heart racing. "I'm honored, sir. But may I ask why me?"

The man – he had introduced himself only as "Smith" – studied Jacob for a long moment. "You're young, educated, and from what we understand, uniquely motivated. Your background, your language skills, your... personal connections to the situation in Europe. All of these make you an ideal candidate for the kind of work we'll be doing."

Jacob's mind flashed to the letters from his cousins in Germany, their words growing more frightened, more desperate with each passing month. He thought of the newsreels he'd seen, the reports filtering out of occupied Europe.

"I'll do it," Jacob said firmly. "Whatever it takes."

Smith nodded, seemingly satisfied. "Very well. From this moment forward, you are no longer Jacob Heller. You are now Jack Holloway. Your training begins immediately. It will be long, it will be hard, and it will prepare you for things you can't even imagine right now."

As Jack left the office, his mind whirling with the enormity of what lay ahead, he felt a strange mix of fear and exhilaration. He was leaving behind everything he had ever known, stepping into a world of shadows and danger.

Jacob Heller had been a young man unsure of his place in the world. Jack Holloway would become a key player in a war fought in the shadows, a war that would shape the future of the world.

ⵣⵣⵣ

The seeds of resistance, planted in moments of darkness and despair, were beginning to take root. In hidden cellars and quiet cafés, in the halls of power and the fields of rural France, a network was forming. A web of courage and determination that would, in time, help topple an empire built on hatred and fear.

Eduard Dupont, the reluctant collaborator turned secret resistance leader. Jack Holloway, the American operative leaving behind his very identity to fight for a cause bigger than himself. Marianne Dupont, the young woman thrust into a world of shadows and danger, carrying the hopes of a nation on her shoulders.

Their paths would soon converge, their fates intertwining in ways none of them could have imagined. Together, they would face challenges that would test the very limits of human endurance. They would know triumph and tragedy, love and loss, moments of soaring hope and crushing despair.

But through it all, they would keep fighting. For France. For freedom. For a future where the dark night of occupation would be nothing more than a distant memory.

The stage was set. The players were in motion. And as the plans were laid for the greatest invasion in history, the first stirrings of a storm that would change the course of history could be felt across occupied France.

1

Descent into Darkness

The night air rushed past Jack Holloway's face as he plummeted through the inky blackness. The drone of aircraft engines faded above him, replaced by the whistle of wind through his parachute straps. His heart pounded in his chest, a thunderous rhythm that seemed to echo across the moonlit French countryside sprawling beneath him.

Just another jump, he told himself. Just like training.

But even as the thought formed, Jack knew it was a lie. This wasn't training. This was Occupied France, late November 1943, and every shadow on the ground could hide a German patrol ready to gun him down the moment his feet touched soil. The weight of his mission pressed down on him, as tangible as the gear strapped to his body.

Jack flexed his fingers, willing feeling back into them as he guided his chute. The thin air at 1000 feet was crisp and biting, carrying the scent of approaching winter. Somewhere below, a family might be huddled around a hearth, unaware that history was dropping out of the sky above their heads. The thought sent a chill through him that had nothing to do with the cold.

He could make out the silvery ribbon of a river, snaking between darker patches he guessed were forests and fields. The OSS had chosen this drop zone for its remoteness, far from major roads or German garrisons. If everything went according to plan, Jack would link up with the local Resistance within hours and begin laying the groundwork for the operations to come in the new year.

If everything went according to plan. Jack had stopped believing in plans the moment he'd stepped off the plane. Too many variables, too many things that could go wrong. He'd seen it before, during his training and in the reports from other operatives. The best-laid plans often went to hell the moment boots hit the ground.

A sudden updraft caught his chute, and he fought to correct his descent. As he wrestled with the lines, memories of the past year and a half flashed through his mind. The grueling training, the endless drills, the punishing physical regimen, the countless hours spent studying maps and memorizing codes. All of it leading to this moment, this leap into the unknown.

As he regained control, a flicker of movement caught his eye. There – to the east. Flashlights, sweeping back and forth across the ground. German voices carried on the wind, barking orders.

Damn it all to hell.

This wasn't just a random patrol. They knew. Somehow, the Germans knew the OSS was coming. Jack's mind raced through the implications, each worse than the last. Had their radio operator been compromised? Was there a mole in the Resistance? Or had they simply been careless, leaving too obvious a trail for Nazi intelligence to follow?

It didn't matter now. All that mattered was getting down and away before –

The crack of gunfire split the night. Bullets whizzed past, punching holes through Jack's chute. He went into a wild spin, the horizon blurring into a dizzying swirl of darkness and stars. The ground rushed up to meet him with terrifying speed.

Jack fought down the surge of panic, forcing himself to focus. He'd trained for this. Twisting his body, he managed to slow the spin. The ground was coming up fast – too fast. He bent his knees, preparing for impact.

He slammed into the earth with bone-jarring force. Pain exploded through his left leg as it buckled beneath him. Jack bit back a scream, tasting blood where he'd bitten his tongue. He rolled, letting his momentum carry him into the cover of bushes lining the field. His hands scrabbled desperately at the chute's release catch.

The sound of German voices grew louder, punctuated by the crackle of radio static. Jack's mind raced, calculating distances, estimating how much time he had before they were on top of him. Not long. Not nearly long enough.

Finally, the harness came free. Jack army-crawled deeper into the brush, thorns tearing at his face and hands. Every movement sent fresh waves of agony through his leg. Gritting his teeth, he forced himself to keep moving. He'd come too far, risked too much, to be captured now.

The beam of a flashlight swept over his hiding spot. Jack froze, not daring to breathe. He could hear the crunch of boots on gravel, coming closer. Closer. The acrid smell of cigarette smoke drifted on the night air, mixed with the sharp scent of gun oil and sweat.

"Hier drüben!" a voice shouted. "I see something!"

Jack's hand crept to the Colt 1911 strapped to his thigh. Seven rounds, he thought grimly. Make them count. Images flashed through his mind – his training, his team, the faces of those depending on him back in London. He couldn't fail them. Wouldn't fail them.

He watched as the beam of light danced ever closer to his position. Jack's finger tightened on the trigger. In that moment, a strange calm settled over him. If this was how it ended, he'd make damn sure to take a few Nazis with him. He steadied his breathing, ready to spring into action.

The light fell directly on the bush concealing him. Jack tensed, ready to spring up firing –

And then the oddest sound cut through the night. A woman's voice, sharp with annoyance, speaking rapid-fire French. Jack's grasp of the language was rudimentary at best, but he caught snatches: "... my father's vineyard... have no right... file a complaint..."

The German voices responded, their tone shifting from predatory excitement to confusion and growing frustration. Jack hardly dared to hope, but the flashlight beam swung away from his hiding place. He held his breath, scarcely believing his luck.

"Fräulein, you do not understand the danger –" one of the German soldiers began in thickly accented French.

"I understand that it is well past curfew," the woman cut him off, "and that you are trespassing. My father will hear of this, and so will your kommandant!"

There was a long, tense moment of silence. Jack could almost feel the indecision radiating from the German soldiers. Then the officer barked an order, and Jack heard the sound of retreating footsteps. He waited, scarcely breathing, for what felt like hours. Slowly, the night settled back into quiet, broken only by the chirping of crickets and the rustle of leaves in the breeze.

"They are gone," the woman's voice came softly, much closer now. "You can come out. Slowly. I have a gun, and I'm not afraid to use it."

Jack weighed his options. Every instinct screamed at him to stay hidden, to trust no one. And yet... this woman had just saved his life. If she'd wanted to turn him in, she'd had ample opportunity. Still, caution won out. He remained silent, watching, waiting.

"I know you're there, American," the woman spoke again, her voice a mixture of impatience and amusement. "Your parachute is hanging from the tree above you. Not very subtle, I'm afraid."

Damn. Jack grimaced, realizing his mistake. So much for a covert insertion. Grimacing against the pain in his leg, he dragged himself out of the bushes. He looked up to find himself staring down the barrel of an old hunting rifle. Behind it stood a young woman, her face half-hidden in shadow. Even in the dim moonlight, he could see the determination in her eyes.

"My name is Jack Holloway," he said, keeping his hands visible. "I'm an American. I'm here to help."

The woman's grip on the rifle didn't waver. "Prove it," she said.

Jack slowly reached into his jacket, withdrawing a small cloth-wrapped package. He heard the woman's sharp intake of breath as he unfolded it, revealing a brilliantly colored silk scarf – blue, white, and red. The recognition signal they'd been told to use.

"Vive la France libre," Jack said softly, the words feeling strange on his tongue.

The woman lowered her rifle, the tension draining from her shoulders. "Thank God," she breathed. "We've been waiting for you." She knelt beside him, her face coming into clearer view. Despite the gravity of the situation, Jack found himself struck by her beauty – delicate features framed by dark curls that had escaped from a simple bun.

"I'm Marianne Dupont," she said, already examining his injured leg with gentle fingers. "And you, Monsieur Holloway, have landed in the middle of my family's vineyard. Welcome to Château Espérance."

Jack managed a weak smile, trying to ignore the pain shooting through his leg. "Hell of a welcoming committee you've got here, Mademoiselle Dupont."

Marianne's answering smile was tight, but there was a glimmer of amusement in her eyes. "Yes, well, we French do like to make an impression." Her expression grew serious once more. "That leg is badly sprained, possibly broken. We need to get you hidden before those Nazi pigs come back with reinforcements."

She stood, slinging the rifle over her shoulder before offering Jack her hand. He took it, marveling at the strength in her grip as she helped him to his feet. Jack leaned heavily on her, trying to keep weight off his injured leg.

As they made their way through the vineyard, Jack's training kicked in. He scanned their surroundings constantly, alert for any sign of danger. But his mind was also racing, trying to piece together the implications of what had just happened. The Germans had known about the drop – that much was clear. But how? And what did it mean for the rest of his team?

Marianne seemed to sense his unease. "Your men," she said softly. "There were others, yes?"

Jack nodded, his jaw tight. "Four others. We were supposed to rendezvous at a safe house about five kilometers from here. But if the Germans knew about the drop..."

He didn't need to finish the thought. Marianne's expression darkened. "We'll find them," she said with quiet determination. "The Resistance has eyes and ears everywhere. If your men are out there, we'll bring them in."

As they walked, Marianne cast a sidelong glance at Jack. "You're younger than I expected," she remarked softly. "When we heard an American captain was coming, I imagined someone... older."

Jack looked up, catching the shadow of doubt in her eyes. He gave a small, rueful smile. "I get that a lot," he admitted. "But I've been training for this with every fiber of my being. I'm ready."

Marianne's eyes searched his face in the dim light, noting the fine lines of tension around his mouth and the determination that burned in his eyes. He may have been young, but there was something about him – a gravity, a depth – that spoke of experiences beyond his years.

"I didn't mean to offend," she said, her tone softening. "It's just... this isn't a game. The stakes are life and death."

Jack shook his head, grimacing as a fresh wave of pain shot through his leg. "No offense taken. I know the risks. I've seen the reports, heard the stories. I'm here to do my part, whatever it takes."

Marianne studied him for a moment longer, then nodded, seeming to come to a decision. "Very well, Captain Holloway," she said, her voice firm. "Let's get you inside. My father will want to meet the man we've been waiting for."

They reached the bottom of a set of worn stone steps leading down to what looked like a cellar entrance. Marianne pushed open the heavy door, revealing a dimly lit room lined with oak barrels and stacks of wooden crates. The faint smell of wine and earth filled the air, mingling with the sharper scent of antiseptic from a makeshift medical station set up in one corner.

As Jack limped into the cellar, leaning heavily on Marianne, he felt a strange mix of relief and apprehension wash over him. He was safe, for now. But the real challenges – finding his team, linking up with the Resistance, carrying out their mission – were just beginning.

The door closed behind them with a soft thud, shutting out the dangerous night. But as Jack looked around at the shadowy cellar, filled with strangers and uncertainty, he couldn't shake the feeling that he had just crossed a threshold into a world far more complex and perilous than anything he'd trained for.

2
Broken Landing

"You are fortunate, Monsieur Holloway," Eduard said, his accent thicker than his daughter's. "It is not broken, merely a bad sprain. But you will not be running from Nazis anytime soon, I'm afraid."

Jack managed a wry smile. "Wasn't planning on much running, to be honest. More of a 'shoot the bastards' kind of mission."

Eduard's eyes crinkled with amusement, but Marianne shot Jack a sharp look. "Perhaps it is best not to discuss your... intentions... quite so openly, Monsieur."

"Right," Jack said, chastened. "Sorry. Guess I'm still a bit rattled from the jump."

"Understandable," Eduard said, beginning to wrap Jack's ankle tightly. "It is not every day one falls from the sky into a war zone, no? But come, you must be hungry. Marianne, would you fetch our guest some bread and cheese? And perhaps a bottle of the '37 Cabernet – for medicinal purposes, of course."

Marianne nodded and slipped away into the shadowy recesses of the cellar. Jack watched her go, struck again by the grace of her movements. He turned back to find Eduard regarding him with a knowing look.

"My daughter is beautiful, yes?" the older man said. "But I warn you, Monsieur Holloway – she is as fierce as she is lovely. Like her mother." A shadow of old grief passed over Eduard's face.

"I'm sorry," Jack said quietly. "The war?"

Eduard shook his head. "No, no. Cancer, three years before the Germans came. In some ways, a blessing. Marie-Claire did not live to see our beloved France fall." He finished wrapping Jack's ankle and sat back. "There. How does it feel?"

Jack gingerly flexed his foot. The pain was still there, a dull throb, but the wrapping provided welcome support. "Better," he said. "Thank you."

Marianne returned, bearing a tray laden with crusty bread, several kinds of cheese, and a dusty bottle of wine. She set it down on a nearby barrel, then poured three glasses of the deep red liquid.

"A toast," Eduard said, raising his glass. "To new friends, and to a free France."

They clinked glasses, and Jack took a sip. The wine was exquisite, rich and complex. He savored it for a moment before setting the glass aside. As much as he wanted to lose himself in the warmth of the alcohol, he needed to keep a clear head.

"I hate to spoil the mood," he said, "but we need to talk about what happened up there. The Germans knew we were coming. Someone tipped them off."

The easy camaraderie of a moment ago evaporated. Marianne and Eduard exchanged a worried glance.

"Are you certain?" Marianne asked. "Could it not have been simply bad luck? A patrol in the wrong place at the wrong time?"

Jack shook his head. "No. They were too prepared, too focused. They knew exactly where to look." He leaned forward, fixing them both with an intense gaze. "I need to know – is there anyone in your Resistance cell who might have German sympathies? Anyone new, or someone acting suspiciously?"

"Impossible," Eduard said firmly. "We have known each other for years. Many of us grew up together in this very village. There is no traitor among us."

"Papa," Marianne said gently, "we must consider every possibility. What about Marcel? He has been... unstable since his brother was taken."

Eduard's face darkened. "Marcel is grieving, yes. But he would never betray us to the Boches. Never."

Jack held up a hand. "Look, I'm not accusing anyone. But the fact remains – somehow, the Germans knew. And if there's a leak, we need to plug it fast. Otherwise, this whole operation is blown before it even starts."

Marianne nodded slowly. "You are right, of course. We will make discreet inquiries, see if anyone has noticed anything unusual." She hesitated, then asked, "What of your team, Monsieur Holloway? You said there were five of you?"

The reminder sent a fresh wave of guilt and worry through Jack. He'd been so focused on his own survival, he'd barely spared a thought for his men. "Yeah," he said heavily. "Lieutenant Mike Carpenter — my second in command. Sergeant Tom O'Brien, radio operator. Corporal David Chen, demolitions expert. And Private First Class Billy Johanssen... just a kid, really. Barely 19."

"And you have heard nothing from them?" Eduard asked.

Jack shook his head. "Radio silence was part of the mission protocol. We weren't supposed to make contact until we'd reached the rendezvous point." He scrubbed a hand over his face, suddenly feeling the weight of every sleepless hour, every mile traveled. "God, for all I know, they could be dead. Or captured. And here I am, drinking wine in a cellar."

Marianne laid a comforting hand on his arm. "Do not despair, Monsieur Holloway. As I said before, our people are searching. If your men are out there, we will find them."

Jack nodded, but the gnawing worry remained. He'd trained with these men, lived with them, shared their hopes and fears. The thought of abandoning them to whatever fate awaited OSS operatives in Nazi hands...

A sudden commotion from above broke through his dark thoughts. Footsteps pounded on the floor overhead, and a voice called out urgently in French.

Eduard was on his feet in an instant, hand reaching for an ancient-looking pistol hidden behind a wine rack. Marianne, too, had produced a weapon from somewhere — this time a more modern Sten submachine gun. Jack reached for his own sidearm, but Marianne shook her head.

"Wait here," she said. "If it is the Germans, we will hold them off as long as we can. There is a hidden door behind that rack — it leads to old smuggling tunnels. Use them to escape if you must."

Before Jack could protest, she and Eduard had slipped out of the cellar, leaving him alone with nothing but the silent ranks of wine bottles for company. He listened intently, straining to make out any sound of conflict from above. His hand stayed near his Colt, ready to draw at a moment's notice.

Long minutes ticked by. Jack's imagination conjured images of firefights raging through the château, of Marianne and Eduard being marched away at gunpoint. He was just about to say to hell with caution and go investigate when the cellar door opened once more.

Marianne entered first, followed by Eduard and two men Jack didn't recognize. But it was the figure they supported between them that drew his attention — a battered, bloodied form in the remnants of an American uniform.

"Mike!" Jack exclaimed, lurching to his feet despite the pain in his ankle. "Jesus Christ, what happened to you?"

Lieutenant Mike Carpenter raised his head, managing a weak grin despite his split lip. "Took a bit of a scenic route, Captain," he slurred. "Lovely country you've got here, Mademoiselle. Bit heavy on the Nazi patrols for my taste, though."

They eased Mike down onto the crate Jack had vacated. Up close, the lieutenant looked even worse — his left eye was swollen shut, and dark bruises mottled his jaw. But it was the way he held himself, slightly hunched and protective of his right side, that worried Jack the most.

"Ribs?" he asked quietly.

Mike nodded. "Couple of 'em, I think. Turns out krauts don't much like it when you drop in uninvited."

Marianne was already busy, gathering medical supplies and enlisting one of the newcomers — a stocky, middle-aged man with a neatly trimmed mustache — to help tend to Mike's injuries.

"This is Doctor Renard," she explained as the man began examining Mike with practiced hands. "And this," she gestured to the other newcomer, a wiry youth barely out of his teens, "is Philippe. He found your lieutenant trying to fight off an entire German patrol single-handedly."

Philippe grinned, revealing a chipped front tooth that gave him a roguish air. "It was most impressive, Monsieur. Like something from the American cinema! But perhaps not very wise, no?"

Mike winced as the doctor probed his ribs. "Yeah, well... seemed like a good idea at the time. They had Johanssen. I couldn't just..."

He trailed off, his good eye clouding with pain — whether physical or emotional, Jack couldn't tell. A chill ran down his spine. "Mike," he said carefully. "What happened to Billy?"

The lieutenant wouldn't meet his gaze. "I'm sorry, Jack. I tried... God, I tried. But there were too many of them. They..." He swallowed hard. "They shot him. Right in front of me. Said it was a message for any other 'terrorists' who might be thinking of causing trouble."

A heavy silence fell over the cellar. Jack felt as if all the air had been sucked out of the room. Billy Johanssen. Nineteen years old. Always quick with a joke, even in the tensest moments. Dreams of going home to Iowa, marrying his high school sweetheart. And now...

"Goddamn it," Jack growled, slamming his fist into the nearby wine rack. Bottles rattled ominously, and Marianne stepped forward, laying a restraining hand on his arm.

"I am so sorry for your loss, Messieurs," she said softly. "But please — we cannot afford to alert anyone to your presence here. The village is crawling with German patrols, all searching for you."

Jack took a deep breath, forcing down the rage and grief that threatened to overwhelm him. She was right, of course. They couldn't afford to lose control now. Too much was at stake.

"What about the others?" he asked Mike. "Carpenter and O'Brien? Any sign of them?"

Mike shook his head. "Nothing. Last I saw, Tom's chute had deployed okay. But David... I think he might've caught some flak on the way down. His chute looked damaged."

"Merde," Eduard muttered. He turned to Philippe. "Go. Find Antoine and the others. Tell them to widen the search area. And for God's sake, be careful. The Germans will be watching for any unusual activity."

Philippe nodded and slipped out of the cellar. Jack watched him go, struck by how young the boy looked. Not much older than Billy had been...

He pushed the thought aside. There would be time to mourn later. Right now, they had a mission to salvage and men to find.

"Alright," he said, forcing himself to focus. "We need to regroup, figure out our next move. Mike, what's our supply situation?"

The lieutenant grimaced as Doctor Renard wrapped his ribs. "Not great, boss. Lost most of my gear during the jump. Got my sidearm, a couple of grenades, and half a chocolate bar. That's about it."

Jack nodded grimly. His own pack was similarly depleted — they'd traveled light, counting on resupply from the local Resistance. A plan that now seemed dangerously optimistic.

"Weapons won't be a problem," Marianne interjected. "We have a cache hidden nearby. Not much, but enough to arm a small team."

"Good," Jack said. "That's something, at least. Now, about this German search pattern — we need to know exactly where they're looking, what kind of manpower they're using. Any chance your people can get eyes on their operations?"

Eduard stroked his mustache thoughtfully. "Perhaps. There is an old fire watchtower on the hill above the village. Long abandoned, but it offers a good view of the surrounding countryside. If we could get someone up there..."

"I'll go," Marianne said immediately.

Her father frowned. "Absolutely not. It's too dangerous."

"Papa," she said, a note of exasperation creeping into her voice, "we have had this argument before. I am not a child to be protected. I am a soldier of the Resistance, just like you."

"She's right," Jack found himself saying. Both Duponts turned to look at him, surprise evident on their faces. "Look, I don't know the terrain, and I'd slow her down with this bum ankle. Marianne's our best bet for getting the intel we need."

Eduard's frown deepened, but after a long moment, he nodded reluctantly. "Very well. But you will take every precaution, you understand? No unnecessary risks."

Marianne's face lit up with a fierce grin. "Of course, Papa. When have I ever taken unnecessary risks?"

The look Eduard gave her suggested this was an old argument, but he didn't press the point. Instead, he turned back to Jack. "And what will you do while my daughter plays lookout?"

Jack considered for a moment. "We need to get a message to our handlers back in London. Let them know the situation, see if they can arrange an emergency extraction for Mike." He glanced at the lieutenant, who was already shaking his head.

"No way, Captain. I'm not leaving you here alone."

"You're in no shape for a firefight, Mike," Jack said firmly. "And if the Germans catch you again..." He left the thought unfinished, but they both knew the implications. The Nazis weren't known for their gentle treatment of captured spies.

Mike looked like he wanted to argue further, but a fresh wave of pain cut him off. He subsided, glowering. "Fine. But I don't like it."

"Noted," Jack said dryly. He turned back to Eduard. "You mentioned a radio operator earlier — Marcel, was it? We need to get in touch with him."

A shadow passed over Eduard's face. "Marcel... may not be in the best state of mind right now. His brother, you see..."

"I know," Jack said gently. "But we don't have a lot of options here. Can you at least ask him?"

Eduard nodded slowly. "I will try. But I make no promises."

"Fair enough." Jack took a deep breath, feeling the weight of command settling onto his shoulders once more. "Alright, here's the plan. Marianne, you head for that watchtower. Get us a clear picture of German movements in the area. Eduard, see if you can raise Marcel on your usual channels. If he's willing to help, great. If not... well, we'll cross that bridge when we come to it."

He turned to Mike, who was looking slightly less pained thanks to whatever the doctor had given him. "You focus on resting up. We're going to need you back on your feet as soon as possible."

"What about you?" Marianne asked.

Jack managed a grim smile. "Me? I'm going to start planning how we're going to rain hell down on every Nazi bastard between here and Paris."

A moment of silence followed his words. Then, to Jack's surprise, Eduard let out a hearty laugh. "I like this one, Marianne," he said, clapping Jack on the shoulder. "He has spirit."

Marianne's eyes met Jack's, and he saw in them a mix of admiration and something else — a spark of connection that sent an unexpected warmth through him. "Yes," she said softly. "He certainly does."

The moment stretched, charged with unspoken possibilities. Then Marianne cleared her throat, breaking the spell. "We should go," she said briskly. "Every minute we delay gives the Germans more time to tighten their net."

Jack nodded, pushing aside the confusing tangle of emotions her gaze had stirred up. There would be time to sort all that out later. Maybe. If they survived.

"Alright, people," he said, falling back on the familiar rhythms of command. "You all know your jobs. Let's move."

As the others filed out of the cellar, leaving him alone with the silent Mike and the ever-present rows of wine bottles, Jack allowed himself a moment of doubt. The mission was in shambles, his team scattered or worse. They were grossly outnumbered and outgunned, deep in enemy territory with no clear extraction plan.

And yet... There was something about this place, these people. The unwavering determination in Marianne's eyes. The quiet strength of Eduard's resolve. Even young Philippe's reckless courage. It kindled a spark of hope in Jack's chest. Maybe, just maybe, they could pull this off.

Jack shook his head, banishing the doubts. He had a job to do.

"How you holding up, Mike?" he asked, turning to his second-in-command.

The lieutenant grunted, shifting uncomfortably on his makeshift bed. "Been better, boss. But I've been worse, too." He managed a weak grin. "Remember Casablanca?"

Jack chuckled despite himself. "How could I forget? You took on half the Vichy French army with nothing but a broken bottle and that ugly mug of yours."

"Hey now," Mike protested, "the ladies love this mug."

Their laughter faded quickly, replaced by a heavy silence. The weight of their losses, of Billy's death, settled over them like a shroud.

"We'll make them pay, Mike," Jack said softly. "For Billy. For every damn thing they've done to this country. I promise you that."

Mike nodded, his good eye gleaming with a mix of grief and determination. "I know we will, Jack. That's why I followed you into this mess. You always were too stubborn to quit."

Before Jack could respond, the cellar door creaked open. Eduard slipped in, his face grave.

"I've made contact with Marcel," he said without preamble. "He... is not well. The loss of his brother has hit him hard. But he has agreed to help, on one condition."

Jack felt a knot of tension form in his gut. "What condition?"

Eduard sighed heavily. "He wants to join your mission. Says he has nothing left to lose, and he wants to make the Germans pay personally."

"Absolutely not," Jack said immediately. "We can't take a civilian with us, especially not one who's emotionally compromised. It's too dangerous."

"I agree," Eduard said. "But Marcel is... insistent. He says if we don't let him help, he'll go to the Germans and turn himself in. Tell them everything he knows about the Resistance."

The knot in Jack's stomach tightened. "Jesus. He's that far gone?"

Eduard spread his hands helplessly. "Grief does strange things to a man, Monsieur Holloway. And Marcel... he and his brother were very close."

Jack ran a hand through his hair, mind racing. They needed that radio contact with London, but bringing an unstable civilian along on a covert op was a recipe for disaster. And yet, if Marcel made good on his threat...

"Alright," he said finally. "Tell him he can come. But make it clear – he follows my orders to the letter, or I'll personally knock him out and leave him tied up in this cellar. Clear?"

Eduard nodded, relief evident on his face. "I will convey your message. Thank you, Monsieur Holloway. I know this is not ideal, but..."

"Nothing about this situation is ideal," Jack cut him off. "We'll make do. Now, any word from Marianne?"

As if on cue, the cellar door opened again, and Marianne slipped in. Her face was flushed, hair windblown, and there was a wild light in her eyes that sent an unexpected thrill through Jack.

"The Germans are everywhere," she reported breathlessly. "At least two full platoons, maybe more. They're conducting house-to-house searches in the village, and they've set up roadblocks on all the major routes in and out."

Jack cursed under his breath. "Any sign of Tom or David?"

Marianne shook her head. "Nothing definite. But I did see signs of a scuffle near the old mill, about two kilometers east of here. And..." she hesitated.

"What is it?" Jack pressed.

"There were rumors in the village. Whispers of an American captured near the river. They say he was wounded, but alive when the Germans took him."

Hope and dread warred in Jack's chest. If one of his men had been captured alive, there was a chance to rescue them. But the longer they remained in German hands...

"Right," he said, forcing decisiveness into his tone. "We need to move fast. Eduard, get Marcel here with that radio. We'll make contact with London, then plan our next move."

He turned to Marianne. "I need you to gather whatever weapons and supplies you can. And see if you can find us some civilian clothes – we'll blend in better if we're not running around in American uniforms."

Marianne nodded, a fierce smile playing at the corners of her mouth. "Consider it done, Monsieur Holloway."

As she turned to go, Jack called out, "Marianne." She paused, looking back at him. "Be careful out there. Please."

Something softened in her eyes. "Always," she said softly, then slipped out of the cellar.

Jack watched her go, an unfamiliar ache in his chest. He pushed the feeling aside, focusing on the task at hand. There would be time to sort out... whatever this was... later. If they survived.

"You're in trouble, boss," Mike's amused voice broke into his thoughts.

Jack turned to find his lieutenant grinning at him despite his injuries. "What are you talking about?"

Mike's grin widened. "I've seen that look before. Usually right before you do something spectacularly heroic and monumentally stupid."

"Shut up and rest, Lieutenant," Jack grumbled, but there was no heat in it.

The next few hours passed in a blur of activity. Marcel arrived, a gaunt, hollow-eyed man who barely spoke beyond terse acknowledgments of Jack's orders. The radio crackled to life, and Jack found himself engaged in a tense, coded conversation with their handlers in London.

The news wasn't good. The failed drop had compromised more than just their immediate mission. Allied command was scrambling to adjust their plans, and extraction was out of the question for the foreseeable future.

"You're on your own for now, Pegasus," the clipped British voice informed him. "Complete the primary objective if possible, but survival is your top priority. We'll try to arrange supply drops when we can. Good luck, and God speed."

The radio went silent, leaving Jack with a bitter taste in his mouth. He'd known it was a long shot, but some small part of him had hoped for a miracle. A daring rescue, perhaps, or at least the promise of reinforcements.

"Well," Mike said from his cot, "I guess we're well and truly screwed now, huh?"

Jack managed a wry smile. "Now, Lieutenant, is that any way for an officer of the United States Army to talk? We're not screwed. We're... creatively challenged."

Mike snorted, then winced as the movement jarred his ribs. "You always did have a way with words, boss."

Before Jack could reply, Marianne returned, laden with an assortment of weapons and clothes. She dumped them on a nearby crate, then turned to Jack with a triumphant grin.

"I hope you gentlemen don't mind smelling like fish," she said. "The only clothes I could find on short notice belonged to old Pierre, the fishmonger."

Jack rifled through the pile, pulling out a worn but serviceable pair of trousers and a patched jacket. "Beggars can't be choosers," he said. "Good work, Marianne."

She beamed at the praise, and Jack felt that now-familiar warmth in his chest. He cleared his throat, forcing himself to focus. "Alright, let's go over what we know. Mike, you feeling up to joining the strategy session?"

The lieutenant nodded, gingerly pushing himself into a sitting position. "Wouldn't miss it for the world, Captain."

Jack laid out a rough map of the area on a barrel, weighing down the corners with bottles of wine. "Okay, here's the situation. We've got at least two platoons of Germans conducting sweeps of the area. They've got roadblocks here, here, and here." He marked the positions Marianne had reported. "We've got a possible sighting of one of our men near the old mill, and rumors of a captured American by the river."

He looked up, meeting the eyes of each person in the cellar – Mike, battered but determined; Marianne, fierce and ready for action; Eduard, grave but resolute; Marcel, a barely contained bundle of grief and rage.

"Our mission parameters have changed," Jack continued. "London's given us free rein to act as we see fit. Our primary objective remains gathering intel on German troop movements and defensive positions along the coast. But right now, our immediate goals are to evade capture, locate our missing men, and if possible, make the Nazis regret ever setting foot in this country."

He paused, letting his words sink in. "It's going to be dangerous. We're outnumbered, outgunned, and operating with minimal support. Anyone who wants to back out, now's the time. No shame in it."

Silence fell over the cellar. Jack looked at each face in turn, seeing only determination and resolve.

"Alright then," he said, a grim smile tugging at his lips. "Let's get to work. Here's what I'm thinking..."

As Jack laid out his plan, he felt a surge of something he hadn't experienced since the disastrous jump – hope. They were battered, broken, and backed into a corner. But looking at the faces around him, the fierce determination in their eyes, he knew one thing for certain.

The Nazis had no idea what was about to hit them.

ごごご

24

3

Echoes of the Past

---◦♡◦---

"Forget everything you think you know about war, gentlemen," the gruff voice cut through the stuffy air of the crowded lecture hall. "Where you're going, there are no front lines, no rules of engagement. There's only the mission, and the ever-present risk of capture, torture, or death."

Jack Holloway sat up straighter in his chair, his eyes fixed on the speaker – a weathered man in his fifties with a face etched by years of covert operations. Colonel William Donovan, head of the newly formed Office of Strategic Services, commanded the room with an intensity that made even the most battle-hardened soldiers among them shift uncomfortably.

"You've been chosen for this program because you possess skills our country desperately needs," Donovan continued, his gaze sweeping across the assembled recruits. "Languages, technical expertise, a knack for thinking on your feet. But make no mistake – what we're about to teach you will push you to your limits and beyond."

Jack felt a mixture of pride and apprehension wash over him. He'd volunteered for this assignment, driven by a burning desire to make a difference in the war effort. But now, faced with the reality of what lay ahead, he couldn't help but wonder if he was in over his head.

The Colonel's voice snapped him back to attention. "Over the next six months, you'll be trained in every aspect of clandestine operations. Intelligence gathering, sabotage, hand-to-hand combat, explosives – by the time you're done, you'll be able to wreak havoc behind enemy lines with nothing more than a paperclip and a stick of chewing gum."

A ripple of nervous laughter went through the room, quickly silenced by Donovan's steely glare. "This isn't a joke, gentlemen. The fate of the free world may very well rest on your ability to operate undetected in occupied territory. You'll be working with resistance groups, coordinating sabotage efforts, and providing crucial intelligence for Allied operations. One mistake, one moment of carelessness, and you could compromise not only your own life but the lives of countless others."

Jack felt the weight of responsibility settle onto his shoulders. He glanced around at his fellow recruits – men from all walks of life, united by their commitment to the cause. He wondered how many of them would make it through the grueling training ahead, how many would survive the dangerous missions that awaited them.

As Donovan launched into a detailed overview of the OSS structure and objectives, Jack's mind drifted back to the day he'd been recruited. It had been just weeks after Pearl Harbor, the nation still reeling from the sudden entry into the war. He'd been working as a translator for a New York publishing house, his facility with languages – particularly German and French – honed by years of study and his own immigrant background.

The man who'd approached him had been nondescript, easily forgettable – exactly the type, Jack would later learn, that made for an effective intelligence operative. He'd spoken of a new agency, one that would operate in the shadows to undermine Nazi control in occupied Europe. The work would be dangerous, he'd said, but vital to the war effort.

Jack had signed up on the spot, driven by a complex mix of patriotism, a desire for adventure, and a deep-seated need to prove himself. Now, listening to Donovan outline the challenges ahead, he felt a renewed sense of purpose. This was his chance to make a real difference, to use his skills in service of a cause greater than himself.

The rest of that first day passed in a blur of lectures and introductions. They were divided into smaller groups based on their anticipated roles – Jack found himself with a cohort of fellow linguists and cultural specialists, many of whom would be tasked with working directly with resistance groups in occupied countries.

It was in one of these smaller sessions that Jack first met Mike Carpenter, a wiry Texan with a quick wit and an uncanny talent for picking locks. "Looks like we'll be spending a lot of time together," Mike drawled as they paired up for a practice exercise in Morse code. "Hope you're ready for some late nights and sore fingers."

Jack grinned, already warming to the other man's easy-going nature. "Bring it on. I've got calluses from years of typing – this should be a breeze."

As it turned out, Morse code was just the beginning. Over the next few weeks, Jack and his fellow recruits were put through a punishing regimen of physical and mental challenges. They learned hand-to-hand combat techniques, practiced marksmanship with a dizzying array of weapons, and spent long hours hunched over radio sets, practicing the art of secure communication.

But it was the more specialized training that really captured Jack's imagination. They learned the intricacies of creating and maintaining cover identities, studied the art of disguise, and were drilled in techniques for resisting interrogation. Jack found himself particularly fascinated by the lessons in cryptography and the use of invisible inks – the idea of hiding crucial information in plain sight appealed to both his linguistic background and his growing appreciation for the subtleties of espionage.

One crisp autumn morning, about a month into their training, Jack and Mike found themselves trudging through the woods of rural Virginia, part of a exercise in evasion and survival. They'd been "dropped" in unfamiliar territory with minimal supplies and told to make their way to an extraction point while avoiding capture by their instructors playing the role of enemy patrols.

"You know," Mike panted as they scrambled up a steep incline, "when I signed up for this, I pictured myself sipping cognac in Paris cafes, charming information out of beautiful enemy agents. Nobody mentioned anything about eating bugs and sleeping in mud."

Jack chuckled, pausing to check their crude map. "Come on, where's your sense of adventure? This is all part of the experience. Besides, I have a feeling the real thing will be a lot less comfortable than this."

Mike's response was cut short by a sudden rustling in the underbrush ahead. Both men froze, instinctively dropping into defensive crouches. Jack's hand went to the small pistol at his hip – loaded with blanks for the exercise, but no less nerve-wracking to use.

A figure burst from the foliage, and Jack had a split second to register the "enemy" armband before his training kicked in. He fired two quick shots, the sharp cracks echoing through the forest. The "enemy" soldier dropped, playing his part with dramatic flair.

"Nice shooting, Tex," Mike quipped, his own weapon trained on the surrounding woods. "But I think you just rang the dinner bell for every other 'Nazi' in the area. We better move."

They spent the next few hours in a tense game of cat and mouse, using every trick they'd learned to evade capture. Jack found himself falling into a state of hyper-awareness, every sense attuned to potential threats. It was exhausting, but exhilarating – a taste of what they might face in the field.

As night fell, they finally reached the extraction point – a small clearing where a nondescript truck waited to take them back to base. Their instructor, a taciturn former Army Ranger named Simmons, nodded approvingly as they approached.

"Not bad, gentlemen," he growled. "You managed to complete the objective without getting yourselves killed. Of course, in real life, the stakes will be a hell of a lot higher."

Back at the training facility, over a meal that tasted like ambrosia after two days of field rations, Jack and Mike compared notes with their fellow recruits. Everyone had stories of close calls and lessons learned the hard way. But beneath the fatigue and the jokes, Jack sensed a growing camaraderie – a bond forged by shared challenges and a common purpose.

As the weeks turned into months, the training intensified. They delved deeper into the specific skills they'd need for their assigned roles. For Jack, this meant an increased focus on working with resistance groups. They studied the complex political landscape of occupied Europe, learning about the various factions and ideologies that drove resistance movements.

One lecture in particular stood out in Jack's memory. The speaker was a French expatriate, a former member of the resistance who had escaped to England after a close call with the Gestapo. His face was gaunt, his eyes haunted by memories of what he'd endured.

"The resistance is not a monolith," he told them, his accented English carrying the weight of hard-won experience. "You will encounter communists, monarchists, ardent patriots, and simple people who just want to protect their homes and families. Your job will be to unite them, to channel their efforts in support of Allied objectives. It will not be easy."

He went on to describe the daily realities of life in occupied France – the constant fear, the shortages, the small acts of defiance that could lead to brutal reprisals. Jack found himself captivated, already imagining the challenges he might face.

"Above all," the Frenchman concluded, "remember that these people are risking everything to fight for their freedom. Treat them with respect, earn their trust, and they will move heaven and earth to help you succeed."

As their training neared its end, the recruits were subjected to increasingly realistic simulations. They practiced parachute jumps, ran complex sabotage operations against mock targets, and endured grueling interrogation sessions designed to test their ability to maintain cover under pressure.

It was during one of these exercises that Jack had a moment of clarity about the path he'd chosen. He was "undercover" in a simulated French village, trying to make contact with a local resistance cell. As he moved through the streets, hyper-aware of the instructors posing as German patrols, he felt a strange sense of rightness settle over him.

This was what he was meant to do. Not just translate documents or relay messages, but to be on the ground, making a tangible difference in the fight against tyranny. The risks were enormous, the potential for failure ever-present. But in that moment, Jack knew with absolute certainty that he was ready to face whatever challenges lay ahead.

The final week of training was devoted to specialized skills relevant to their individual assignments. For Jack, this meant intensive work on radio operation and cryptography. He spent long hours hunched over complex coding machines, learning to encrypt and decrypt messages with speed and accuracy.

"Remember," their instructor emphasized, "in the field, time will always be against you. A few seconds delay in decoding a message could mean the difference between success and catastrophic failure."

They also received crash courses in the latest sabotage techniques. Jack was fascinated by the ingenuity of the devices they were shown – explosives disguised as lumps of coal, incendiary pencils that could be used to start fires, even rats stuffed with plastic explosives, designed to be placed in Nazi boilers.

"The key," their demolitions expert explained, "is to create maximum disruption with minimum risk of civilian casualties. We're not here to terrorize the population – our targets are military and industrial infrastructure."

On their last night at the training facility, Colonel Donovan himself addressed the graduating class. His words were solemn, impressing upon them the gravity of the task ahead.

"You are about to embark on missions that will test you in ways you can't yet imagine," he said. "You will face danger, privation, and moral dilemmas that would break lesser men. But know this – the work you do, the risks you take, will save countless lives and bring us closer to victory."

He paused, his gaze sweeping across the assembled operatives. "Some of you will not return. That is the harsh reality of the work we do. But those who do will have the satisfaction of knowing they played a crucial role in defeating one of the greatest evils the world has ever known."

As Donovan's words sank in, Jack felt a complex mix of emotions – pride, apprehension, determination. He glanced at Mike, saw the same resolve mirrored in his friend's eyes. Whatever lay ahead, they would face it together, armed with the skills and knowledge imparted to them over these grueling months.

Later that night, unable to sleep, Jack found himself walking the grounds of the facility one last time. The moon hung low and full, casting long shadows across the familiar landscape. In just a few short days, he would be on a plane bound for England, and from there, into the heart of occupied France.

He thought about his family – the parents who had fled Germany years ago, seeking a better life in America. What would they think of their son, willingly heading into the very danger they had escaped? He hadn't been able to tell them the full truth of his assignment, of course. As far as they knew, he was joining a special military intelligence unit. It wasn't entirely a lie, but the gulf between that sanitized description and the reality of what he was about to undertake felt vast.

Jack's reflections were interrupted by the sound of approaching footsteps. He turned to see Mike ambling towards him, hands stuffed in his pockets.

"Couldn't sleep either, huh?" the Texan drawled.

Jack shook his head. "Too much on my mind, I guess. Trying to wrap my head around what we're about to do."

Mike nodded, his usual joking manner replaced by a more serious mien. "Yeah, I know what you mean. It's one thing to train for this stuff, another thing entirely to actually do it."

They stood in companionable silence for a moment, each lost in their own thoughts. Finally, Mike spoke again. "Listen, Jack. I know we've only known each other a few months, but I want you to know – there's no one I'd rather have watching my back out there than you."

Jack felt a lump form in his throat. "Thanks, Mike. I feel the same way."

They clasped hands, the gesture carrying the weight of a solemn vow. Whatever challenges lay ahead, whatever dangers they might face, they would face them together – as comrades, as brothers in arms.

As the first light of dawn began to paint the eastern sky, Jack took a deep breath, squaring his shoulders. The long months of training were behind them. The real work – the dangerous, vital work of undermining Nazi control and paving the way for liberation – was about to begin.

He was ready. Not fearless, certainly – only a fool would be fearless in the face of what they were about to undertake. But prepared. Determined. Committed to the cause that had brought him to this point.

As he and Mike turned to head back to their quarters, Jack allowed himself one last glance at the facility that had been their home for the past six months. So much had changed since he'd first arrived – not just in terms of skills and knowledge, but in his very sense of self. He was no longer just Jack Holloway, translator and reluctant desk jockey. He was an OSS operative, trained and ready to take the fight directly to the enemy.

The sun crested the horizon, its rays catching the dew on the grass and turning the world to gold. A new day was dawning – for Jack, for the OSS, for the entire war effort. And with it came the promise of action, of purpose, of a chance to make a real difference in the struggle against tyranny.

Whatever lay ahead, Jack knew one thing with absolute certainty – he was exactly where he was meant to be. The echoes of the past – his family's history, his own journey to this point – had led him here. Now it was time to write a new chapter, not just in his own story, but in the grand narrative of the war itself.

With a final nod to Mike, Jack turned and walked purposefully towards the future that awaited them both. The real work was about to begin.

ppp

4

Silent Pursuit

"They're moving," Marianne whispered, lowering her binoculars. "Two trucks, heavily guarded. Heading east."

Jack's jaw tightened. "Towards the château?"

"Looks like it. We've got maybe an hour before they reach it."

"Then we'd better move fast," Jack replied, his mind already racing with plans.

The pre-dawn air was crisp and heavy with dew as Jack and Marianne crouched among the gnarled vines of Château Espérance. Jack's borrowed clothes itched, the rough fabric a far cry from his usual uniform. But discomfort was a small price to pay for anonymity.

Marianne's dark eyes scanned the misty rows of grapes stretching out before them. "The regular patrols will come through just after sunrise," she added. "We should have about an hour before we need to worry about them too."

Jack nodded, adjusting the unfamiliar weight of the Sten gun slung across his back. The weapon was a far cry from his trusty M1, but beggars couldn't be choosers. And right now, they were begging for every advantage they could get.

"Alright," he murmured. "Let's go over the plan one more time."

Marianne rolled her eyes, but there was a hint of a smile playing at the corners of her mouth. "We've been over it three times already, Monsieur Holloway. Are all American officers so thorough, or is it just you?"

"Humor me," Jack said, fighting back a grin of his own. "And please, call me Jack. I think we're a bit past formalities at this point."

She regarded him for a moment, then nodded. "Very well... Jack. The plan, once again, is this: We make our way to the old mill, where you believe your radioman might be hiding. If we find him, we bring him back to the château. If not, we search for clues about his whereabouts or the location of your other missing man."

"And if we run into trouble?" Jack prompted.

"We use the pre-arranged signals to alert the others," Marianne continued. "Two short whistles for 'danger approaching,' three for 'immediate assistance needed.' Eduard and Marcel will be positioned here and here" — she pointed to spots on a crude map drawn in the dirt — "ready to provide cover fire or a distraction if necessary."

Jack nodded, satisfied. It wasn't much of a plan, but it was the best they could do with limited resources and even more limited time. Every moment they delayed increased the risk of the Germans finding their hideout or capturing — or killing — more of his men.

"Okay," he said. "Let's move out."

They rose in unison, hunched low to avoid presenting easy targets in the early morning light. Jack's injured ankle protested as he put weight on it, but he gritted his teeth and pushed through the pain. He couldn't afford to be slowed down now.

As they made their way through the vineyard, Jack found his gaze continually drawn to Marianne. She moved with a fluid grace, every step sure and purposeful. It was clear she knew this land intimately — every dip, every rise, every potential hiding spot.

"You've lived here your whole life?" he asked softly as they paused behind a weathered stone wall.

Marianne nodded, a distant look in her eyes. "Since I was born. This land... it's more than just soil and vines. It's history. My family's history." She ran a hand along the rough stone. "My great-grandfather built this wall with his own hands. Every vintage, every harvest... they're all part of us."

Jack felt a pang of something — envy? regret? — at the depth of connection she clearly felt to this place. "Must be nice," he said. "Having roots like that."

She turned to look at him, curiosity evident in her gaze. "And you, Jack? Where do you call home?"

He shrugged, suddenly uncomfortable. "Nowhere, really. Army brat. Moved around so much as a kid, I never really put down roots anywhere."

"That sounds... lonely," Marianne said softly.

Jack was saved from having to respond by a distant sound — the rumble of engines. They both tensed, pressing themselves flat against the wall.

"Truck," Marianne whispered. "Coming from the village. We need to move."

They hurried on, keeping low and using the vineyard's natural contours for cover. As they neared the edge of the Dupont property, the dilapidated form of the old mill came into view. Its weathered wooden sides and sagging roof spoke of years of neglect, but to Jack, it looked like salvation. If Tom had made it this far...

A sharp crack split the air — a twig snapping underfoot. Jack and Marianne froze, eyes scanning their surroundings. For a long, tense moment, nothing moved.

Then, from the shadows of a nearby copse of trees, a figure emerged. Jack's hand went to his weapon, but Marianne laid a restraining hand on his arm.

"Wait," she hissed. "I know him."

The figure drew closer, resolving into a young man — barely more than a boy, really. His clothes were dirty and torn, and he moved with the wary caution of a hunted animal. But as he caught sight of Marianne, his face lit up with relief.

"Mademoiselle Dupont!" he called softly. "Thank God. I've been hiding out here all night, afraid to move."

Marianne hurried to the boy's side, Jack following close behind. "Pierre," she said, "what are you doing out here? It's not safe."

The boy — Pierre — nodded vigorously. "I know, I know. But I had to tell someone. The Americans — I saw them!"

Jack's heart leapt. "Where?" he demanded, perhaps more forcefully than he intended. Pierre took a step back, eyes widening as he noticed Jack for the first time.

Marianne laid a calming hand on the boy's shoulder. "It's alright, Pierre. This is... a friend. Tell us what you saw."

Pierre swallowed hard, then nodded. "It was last night. I was coming back from checking my snares in the woods — I know I'm not supposed to be out after curfew," he added quickly, seeing Marianne's frown. "But with the rationing, we needed the meat. Anyway, I was near the river when I heard shouting. German shouting."

Jack and Marianne exchanged a glance. This matched the rumors they'd heard about a captured American.

"Go on," Jack urged.

"I hid in the bushes," Pierre continued. "And that's when I saw them. Two men in uniforms I didn't recognize — American uniforms, I guess. One was hurt bad, the other was half-carrying him. They were trying to get away from the Germans, but..." He trailed off, his young face twisted with anguish.

"What happened?" Jack asked, dreading the answer.

"The Germans caught up to them," Pierre said softly. "They shot the injured one. The other... they took him away. I'm sorry, I wanted to help, but there were so many of them..."

Jack closed his eyes, a wave of grief and anger washing over him. Another man lost. And one captured — Tom or David, it had to be. Probably Tom, given the mention of the radio.

"You did the right thing," Marianne was saying to Pierre. "If you'd tried to intervene, you would have been killed too."

Jack took a deep breath, forcing himself to focus. Grieve later. Act now. "Pierre," he said, kneeling down to look the boy in the eye. "This is very important. Do you remember where exactly this happened? Could you show us?"

Pierre nodded hesitantly. "I... I think so. But the Germans — they're still out there, looking."

"We'll be careful," Jack assured him. He looked to Marianne. "This changes things. We need to get word back to Eduard and the others."

Marianne bit her lip, thinking. "Pierre," she said after a moment, "I need you to go back to the château. Tell my father what you've told us. Can you do that?"

The boy straightened, a look of determination replacing his fear. "Yes, Mademoiselle. I can do that."

"Good lad," Jack said. He turned to Marianne as Pierre slipped away, moving with the natural stealth of a boy used to avoiding trouble. "You sure about this? Splitting up isn't ideal."

Marianne met his gaze steadily. "No, it's not. But we don't have much choice. Every minute we delay..."

She didn't need to finish the thought. Jack knew all too well what could happen to a captured operative in German hands. He nodded grimly. "Alright. Lead the way."

They set off again, this time angling towards the river. The sun was climbing higher now, burning off the morning mist and painting the countryside in soft golds and greens. In other circumstances, it might have been beautiful. Now, it just made Jack feel exposed.

As they neared the spot Pierre had described, Marianne suddenly held up a hand, signaling for silence. Jack froze, straining his ears. For a moment, he heard nothing but the gentle burble of the nearby river and the rustle of leaves in the breeze.

Then — voices. German voices, growing closer.

"Patrol," Marianne mouthed silently. She pointed to a dense thicket of bushes. "Hide."

They dove for cover just as two German soldiers rounded a bend in the path. Jack's heart hammered in his chest as he watched through the leaves. The soldiers were young — probably conscripts, barely older than Pierre. They walked with the bored indifference of men pulled away from more interesting duties.

One of them paused, lighting a cigarette. He said something to his companion that made them both laugh. Jack felt Marianne tense beside him, her hand inching towards her weapon.

He laid a restraining hand on her arm, shaking his head slightly. The odds were in their favor, but gunfire would bring every German in the area down on their heads. Better to wait, to let them pass.

Long seconds ticked by. Jack barely dared to breathe. Finally, mercifully, the soldiers moved on, their voices fading into the distance.

Marianne let out a shaky breath. "That was too close," she whispered.

Jack nodded, but his attention was already elsewhere. Now that the immediate danger had passed, he could see signs of the struggle Pierre had described. Trampled undergrowth. A dark stain on a nearby rock that could only be blood.

And there — half-hidden in the mud by the riverbank — a scrap of olive drab fabric.

Jack moved carefully, retrieving the sodden cloth. His stomach clenched as he recognized it — a sleeve torn from an American uniform jacket. And pinned to it, glinting dully in the morning light, was a set of dog tags.

With trembling fingers, he wiped away the mud, revealing the stamped letters:

CHEN, DAVID K.

387-99-4421

O NEG

NO PREFERENCE

"Oh, David," Jack murmured, closing his fist around the tags. Another good man lost. How many more before this mission — this war — was over?

He felt a gentle hand on his shoulder and looked up to find Marianne watching him, her eyes full of sympathy and something else — a fierce determination that stirred an answering fire in his chest.

"We'll make them pay," she said softly. "For your men. For France. For all of it."

Jack nodded, tucking the dog tags into his pocket. "Yes," he said. "We will." He took a deep breath, pushing down the grief and rage. There would be time for that later. Now, they had a job to do.

"Alright," he said, his voice steadier than he felt. "We know David... didn't make it. But Tom's still out there somewhere. Probably being held for interrogation. We need to find out where they'd take him."

Marianne frowned, thinking. "There's a Gestapo headquarters in the next town over. But for an American prisoner... they might take him all the way to Paris."

Jack shook his head. "No, they'll want to question him quickly, get whatever intel they can before moving him. Is there anywhere closer? A temporary base, maybe?"

"There's an old château about ten kilometers from here," Marianne said slowly. "The Nazis requisitioned it when they first arrived. They use it as a local command post."

"That's got to be it," Jack said. He glanced at the sky, gauging the time. "We need to get back, regroup with the others. If we're going to hit a Nazi stronghold, we'll need every hand we can get."

Marianne nodded. "Agreed. But Jack..." She hesitated, then pressed on. "Are you sure about this? It's an enormous risk. If we're caught..."

"I know," Jack said quietly. "But I can't leave him behind. I won't." He met her gaze, willing her to understand. "These men... they're more than just soldiers to me. They're family."

For a long moment, Marianne said nothing. Then, slowly, she nodded. "I understand," she said. "And I'll help you. We all will." A small, fierce smile played at the corners of her mouth. "Besides, it's not every day we get the chance to strike such a blow against the Boche."

Jack felt a surge of gratitude — and something else, something warmer — towards this remarkable woman. "Thank you," he said simply.

They set off back towards Château Espérance, moving as quickly as stealth would allow. As they walked, Jack found his mind racing, already formulating plans and contingencies. It would be dangerous — perhaps the most dangerous thing he'd ever attempted. But looking at Marianne, seeing the determination in her eyes, he felt a spark of hope.

They had a chance. A small one, perhaps, but a chance nonetheless. And sometimes, that was all you needed.

As the familiar slopes of the Dupont vineyard came into view, Jack allowed himself a grim smile. The Nazis thought they had the upper hand. They were about to learn just how wrong they were.

The sanctuary of the vineyard awaited. And beyond it — vengeance, justice, and with luck, salvation for a captured comrade. Jack quickened his pace, Marianne matching him step for step.

ᚦᚦᚦ

5

Whispers Among the Vines

The cellar of Château Espérance was alive with tense energy as Jack Holloway laid out his plan. The faces around him were a study in contrasts: Mike, still pale and drawn from his injuries but with a fierce light in his eyes; Eduard, his weathered features set in grim determination; Marcel, practically vibrating with barely contained rage; and Marianne, her dark eyes meeting Jack's with a mix of admiration and concern.

"It's risky," Jack concluded, running a hand through his hair. "I won't lie to you. If anything goes wrong, we could all end up dead or worse. But it's our best shot at getting Tom out alive."

"And striking a blow against the Boche," Marcel interjected, his voice tight with suppressed emotion. "Don't forget that, American. This isn't just about your man."

Jack nodded, acknowledging the point. "You're right. If we pull this off, we'll be dealing a significant blow to Nazi operations in the area. But make no mistake – our primary objective is rescuing Sergeant O'Brien. Everything else is secondary."

Marcel's eyes flashed dangerously, but before he could speak, Eduard laid a calming hand on his arm. "Peace, my friend," the older man said softly. "Remember why we fight. Not for vengeance alone, but for freedom. For France."

A tense silence fell over the cellar. Jack could practically feel the competing agendas and emotions swirling around him. He knew he was asking a lot of these people – risking their lives for a man they'd never met, for a cause that wasn't entirely their own.

Marianne broke the silence, her voice steady and clear. "I'm in," she said simply. "Whatever it takes."

Jack felt a rush of gratitude – and something more, something he wasn't quite ready to name. He gave her a nod of thanks before turning to the others. "Anyone else?"

"Do you even need to ask, boss?" Mike said with a weak grin. "Wild horses couldn't keep me away. Though... you might need to tie me to the hood of the car or something. Not sure how much running I'll be doing."

"You're staying here, Lieutenant," Jack said firmly. "You're in no shape for a firefight."

Mike opened his mouth to protest, but Eduard cut him off. "He's right, my friend. You need time to heal. But fear not – you can help coordinate from here. We'll need someone to man the radio, keep us informed of any German movements."

The lieutenant didn't look happy about it, but he nodded reluctantly. "Fine. But if you all get yourselves killed, I'm going to be very put out."

"Noted," Jack said dryly. He turned to Eduard and Marcel. "What about you two? I won't order you to come. This isn't your fight."

Eduard straightened, a spark of the old soldier visible in his bearing. "Monsieur Holloway, every fight against the Nazis is our fight. We've been resisting in small ways for years. Now, finally, we have a chance to strike a real blow. Wild horses, as your lieutenant says, could not keep us away."

Marcel nodded in fierce agreement. "For once, the old man and I are in complete agreement. We're with you, American. To whatever end."

Jack felt a swell of emotion in his chest – pride, gratitude, and a fierce determination. These people, virtual strangers just days ago, were willing to risk everything for his mission, for his men. He wouldn't let them down.

"Alright," he said, his voice rough with feeling. "Then let's get to work. We've got a lot to do and not much time to do it in."

The next few hours passed in a flurry of activity. Weapons were cleaned and checked, explosives carefully prepared under Jack's watchful eye. Eduard disappeared into the village, using his network of contacts to gather crucial intelligence on Nazi patrol patterns and the layout of the target château.

As the sun began to set, casting long shadows across the vineyard, Jack found himself alone in the cellar, poring over a crude map of the area. He was so engrossed in his planning that he didn't hear the soft footsteps behind him.

"You should rest," Marianne's voice came softly. "Tomorrow will be long and dangerous. You'll need your strength."

Jack turned, offering her a weary smile. "I will. Just want to go over everything one more time. Make sure we haven't missed anything."

Marianne moved to stand beside him, her shoulder brushing his as she leaned over the map. The contact sent a jolt through Jack, and he found himself acutely aware of her presence – the faint scent of lavender in her hair, the warmth radiating from her body.

"You care for them very much, don't you?" she said softly. "Your men."

Jack nodded, his throat suddenly tight. "They're more than just soldiers to me. They're..." He trailed off, struggling to find the words.

"Family," Marianne finished for him. She laid a gentle hand on his arm. "I understand. It's the same for us here. The Resistance... we're bound by more than just a common cause."

Jack met her gaze, seeing in her eyes a reflection of his own feelings – the weight of responsibility, the fear of loss, the fierce devotion to those who fought beside you. Without thinking, he reached out, covering her hand with his own.

For a long moment, they stood like that, connected by touch and shared understanding. Then, slowly, reluctantly, Jack pulled away. "We should both get some rest," he said, his voice rougher than he'd intended. "Big day tomorrow."

Marianne nodded, a faint flush coloring her cheeks. "Of course. Bonne nuit, Jack. Sleep well."

As she turned to go, Jack called out softly, "Marianne." She paused, looking back at him. "Thank you. For everything."

She gave him a small, warm smile. "Always," she said simply, and then she was gone, leaving Jack alone with his thoughts and the lingering warmth of her touch.

Sleep, when it finally came, was fitful and filled with disjointed dreams. Jack found himself back in Casablanca, running through narrow alleys with unseen enemies at his heels. But when he turned to face his pursuers, it was Billy Johanssen's face he saw, young and accusing. "Why didn't you save me, Captain?" the dead soldier asked. "Why didn't you bring me home?"

Jack woke with a start, heart pounding. The cellar was dark and quiet, the only sound the soft breathing of his sleeping comrades. He lay still for a long moment, willing his racing pulse to slow.

As the first gray light of dawn began to seep through the high windows, Jack rose silently, careful not to wake the others. He made his way up the worn stone steps and out into the vineyard.

The air was cool and misty, heavy with the promise of rain. Jack breathed deeply, letting the clean scent of earth and growing things wash over him. In the distance, a rooster crowed, heralding the coming day.

"Couldn't sleep?" Eduard's voice came softly from behind him.

Jack turned to find the older man leaning against a gnarled old vine, a steaming cup of coffee in his hands. "Bad dreams," Jack admitted. "Ghosts of missions past."

Eduard nodded in understanding. "The price we pay for survival," he said. "Here." He produced another cup of coffee from somewhere and handed it to Jack. "You look like you could use this."

Jack took the cup gratefully, savoring the rich aroma. "Thanks," he said. "How are you holding up? Ready for today?"

A grim smile touched Eduard's lips. "As ready as one can be for such things. It has been... a long time since I've seen combat. But some things, I think, one never forgets."

They stood in companionable silence for a while, sipping their coffee and watching the mist slowly burn away as the sun rose. Finally, Eduard spoke again, his voice low and serious.

"Jack... I must ask you something. And I need you to answer honestly."

Jack turned to face him, sensing the weight behind the words. "Of course. What is it?"

Eduard's eyes, when they met Jack's, were filled with a mixture of concern and steely resolve. "If things go wrong today... if it comes down to a choice between completing the mission and saving my daughter... what will you do?"

The question hit Jack like a physical blow. He opened his mouth to respond, then closed it again, realizing he didn't have an answer. The soldier in him, the part that had been drilled in duty and mission parameters, knew what the "right" answer was. But the man... the man who had felt the warmth of Marianne's touch, who had seen the fire in her eyes...

"I..." Jack began, then stopped, taking a deep breath. "I don't know," he said finally, honestly. "I want to tell you that the mission comes first. That's what I've been trained for, what I've always believed. But Marianne... she's..."

"Special," Eduard finished for him, a knowing look in his eyes. "Yes, I've seen how you look at her. How she looks at you."

Jack felt a flush creep up his neck. "It's not... we haven't..."

Eduard held up a hand, cutting off Jack's stammering. "I am not blind, my friend. Nor am I a fool. Love has a way of blooming even in the darkest times. Perhaps especially then." His expression grew serious once more. "But love can also be a dangerous distraction in our line of work."

"I know," Jack said quietly. "Believe me, I know. But I swear to you, Eduard – I will do everything in my power to keep her safe. To keep all of you safe."

Eduard studied him for a long moment, then nodded slowly. "I believe you," he said. "And I trust you, Jack. With my daughter's life and with the fate of our cause." He clasped Jack's shoulder firmly. "Now come. The others will be waking soon. We have a long day ahead of us."

As they made their way back to the cellar, Jack's mind whirled with conflicting emotions. Eduard's words had brought into sharp focus feelings he'd been trying to ignore – feelings that could complicate an already dangerous mission.

But there was no time for soul-searching now. They had a man to rescue and a Nazi stronghold to infiltrate. Whatever lay between him and Marianne would have to wait.

The cellar was a hive of activity when they returned. Mike was hunched over the radio, fine-tuning the frequencies. Marcel was methodically checking and rechecking their weapons, his face set in grim determination. And Marianne...

Marianne looked up as Jack entered, her eyes finding his across the crowded space. For a moment, the world seemed to fall away, narrowing to just the two of them. Then she gave him a small, fierce smile and a nod, and the spell was broken.

"Alright, people," Jack said, pushing aside his tumultuous emotions and slipping into the familiar role of commander. "This is it. We've been over the plan, but let's run through it one more time. Marianne?"

She stepped forward, unrolling a rough map on a nearby crate. "The target is here," she said, pointing to a spot about 10 kilometers to the east. "It's an old château, built in the 16th century. The Nazis have turned it into a local command post and detention center."

Jack nodded, picking up the thread. "Our intel suggests they're holding Tom – Sergeant O'Brien – in the cellar. Security is tight, but not impenetrable. We'll approach from the north, using the cover of the orchards to get close."

"Marcel and I will create a diversion here," Eduard said, indicating a spot on the map. "A small explosion, nothing too destructive, but enough to draw attention and pull guards away from the main building."

"Meanwhile," Jack continued, "Marianne and I will infiltrate through this old servants' entrance. It's less heavily guarded, and according to Eduard's contacts, the locks are old and easy to pick."

"Once inside," Marianne picked up, "we make our way to the cellar, locate Sergeant O'Brien, and get him out. Fast and quiet."

Jack looked around the room, meeting each pair of eyes in turn. "Make no mistake – this is going to be dangerous. If anyone wants to back out, now's the time. No one will think less of you."

A moment of silence fell over the cellar. Then Marcel stepped forward, his face set in fierce determination. "We're with you, American. To the end."

The others nodded in agreement, and Jack felt a swell of pride and gratitude. "Alright then," he said. "Let's gear up. We move out in 30 minutes."

As the others bustled about, making final preparations, Jack felt a presence at his elbow. He turned to find Marianne standing there, her dark eyes searching his face.

"Are you alright?" she asked softly. "You seem... distracted."

Jack managed a small smile. "Just pre-mission jitters," he lied. "Nothing to worry about."

Marianne didn't look convinced, but she nodded. "Jack," she said, her voice barely above a whisper. "Whatever happens today... I want you to know..."

She trailed off, seeming to struggle for words. Jack felt his heart rate quicken. "What is it?" he prompted gently.

Marianne opened her mouth to respond, but before she could, Marcel's voice cut through the cellar. "Time to go, people! Let's kill some Nazis!"

The moment shattered. Marianne stepped back, the vulnerability in her eyes replaced by steely resolve. "We should go," she said. "Be careful out there, Jack."

"You too," he replied, watching as she turned away to gather her gear.

As Jack did a final check of his own equipment, he couldn't shake the feeling that something fundamental had shifted. The whispers among the vines had grown louder, carrying promises and dangers in equal measure.

ppp

6

The Occupied Cellar

The ancient stones of the château loomed before them, bathed in the pale light of a waning moon. Jack Holloway crouched in the shadows of the orchard, Marianne a silent presence at his side. His heart pounded in his chest, a rhythm of anticipation and fear.

"Two guards at the main gate," Marianne whispered, her breath warm against his ear. "Another patrolling the eastern wall."

Jack nodded, his eyes never leaving the imposing structure. "Eduard and Marcel should be in position by now. We move on their signal."

As if on cue, a muffled explosion rocked the night. Flames blossomed on the far side of the château, followed by shouts of alarm in German. The guards at the gate snapped to attention, their rifles raised.

"That's our cue," Jack murmured. "Let's move."

They darted from shadow to shadow, using the chaos of the diversion to their advantage. Jack's injured ankle protested with each step, but he gritted his teeth and pushed through the pain. Too much was riding on this mission to let a little discomfort slow him down.

They reached the old servants' entrance without incident. Marianne made quick work of the lock, her nimble fingers moving with practiced ease. Jack kept watch, every nerve on high alert.

The door swung open with a faint creak. Jack winced at the sound, but the commotion from the explosion covered it. They slipped inside, finding themselves in a narrow, musty corridor.

"The cellar should be this way," Marianne whispered, pointing down a flight of worn stone steps.

Jack nodded, drawing his pistol. "I'll take point. Watch our six."

They descended into the bowels of the château, the air growing cooler and damper with each step. The sounds of confusion from above became muffled, replaced by an oppressive silence broken only by their careful footsteps and the pounding of Jack's heart in his ears.

At the bottom of the stairs, they found themselves facing a heavy wooden door. Jack pressed his ear against it, straining to hear any sound from the other side. Nothing.

He met Marianne's eyes, saw his own tension mirrored there. With a nod, he gripped the handle and slowly, carefully, eased the door open.

The cellar beyond was a large, vaulted space, dimly lit by a few bare bulbs. Rows of wine racks lined the walls, a reminder of the château's more peaceful past. But it was the center of the room that drew Jack's attention – and made his blood run cold.

Sergeant Tom O'Brien was there, strapped to a chair. His face was a mass of bruises, one eye swollen shut. Blood matted his hair and stained his tattered uniform. But he was alive – Jack could see the shallow rise and fall of his chest.

And he wasn't alone.

A figure in a crisp SS uniform stood over Tom, his back to the door. Even from behind, Jack recognized the casual cruelty in the man's posture, the way he toyed with something in his hands – something that glinted dully in the low light.

"Come now, Sergeant," the SS officer was saying, his German-accented English dripping with false congeniality. "Surely you can see the futility of your situation. Why suffer needlessly? Tell me what I want to know, and all this unpleasantness can end."

Tom raised his head with visible effort. When he spoke, his voice was hoarse but defiant. "Sergeant O'Brien, Thomas P. Serial number 3845627."

The SS officer sighed theatrically. "Very well. If you insist on being difficult..." He raised his hand, and Jack saw what he'd been toying with – a wicked-looking pair of pliers.

Time seemed to slow. Jack knew they had to act now, but the rational part of his mind screamed caution. They were outnumbered, outgunned. One wrong move and they'd all end up dead or worse.

But then Tom's eyes, dazed with pain, drifted past the SS officer – and locked onto Jack's. A flicker of recognition, of hope, passed over the sergeant's battered face.

And just like that, the decision was made.

Jack burst from cover, his pistol raised. "Freeze!" he barked. "Hands where I can see them!"

The SS officer whirled, surprise written across his aristocratic features. For a split second, he stood frozen. Then his hand darted towards the holster at his hip.

Jack didn't hesitate. Two shots rang out, deafeningly loud in the enclosed space. The officer staggered, a look of almost comical disbelief on his face, then crumpled to the ground.

"Clear," Jack called, his voice tight with adrenaline.

Marianne was already moving, securing the door behind them. "We don't have much time," she said urgently. "Someone will have heard those shots."

Jack nodded, holstering his weapon and hurrying to Tom's side. Up close, the sergeant looked even worse. Fresh burns and cuts marred his skin, testament to the ordeal he'd endured.

"Took you long enough, Captain," Tom managed, his split lips twitching in a faint approximation of a smile.

"Yeah, well, you know how I like to make an entrance," Jack replied, his voice rough with emotion as he worked to undo the restraints. "Can you walk?"

Tom grimaced. "Might need a little help, sir. Bastards worked me over pretty good."

"I've got you, buddy," Jack said, slinging Tom's arm over his shoulders. "Let's get the hell out of here."

They had barely taken two steps when the cellar door burst open. A pair of German soldiers rushed in, alerted by the gunshots. For a heartbeat, everyone froze.

Then Marianne was moving, a blur of deadly grace. Her Sten gun chattered, the sound deafening in the enclosed space. The Germans went down in a spray of blood and shattered masonry.

"Move!" Marianne shouted, already turning to cover their retreat.

They staggered towards the exit, Jack half-carrying Tom. Every step sent waves of agony through his injured ankle, but he pushed through it, running on pure adrenaline and determination.

More shouts echoed from above – the entire château was alerted now. They needed to get out, and fast.

They burst out of the servants' entrance into the cool night air. The orchard lay just ahead, promising cover and escape. But between them and safety stretched an exposed stretch of moonlit lawn.

"Go," Marianne urged, her eyes darting between the château and their goal. "I'll cover you."

Jack hesitated, torn between the need to get Tom to safety and an overwhelming reluctance to leave Marianne behind. "I can't just–"

"Go!" she repeated, more forcefully this time. "I'll be right behind you."

There was no time to argue. Jack nodded, tightening his grip on Tom. "Be careful," he said, meeting her eyes one last time.

Then they were running, or as close to running as they could manage with Tom's injuries. Jack's world narrowed to the pounding of his heart, the ragged gasps of Tom's breathing, and the agonizing distance to the treeline.

Behind them, Marianne's Sten gun erupted in short, controlled bursts. German shouts turned to screams of pain and anger.

They were halfway across the lawn when a bullet whizzed past Jack's ear, so close he felt the displacement of air. Another struck the ground at his feet, kicking up a spray of dirt.

"Almost there," he panted, more to himself than to Tom. "Just a little further."

The orchard's shadows loomed ahead, tantalizingly close. Jack's lungs burned, his ankle a white-hot point of agony. But he didn't dare slow down.

Ten more steps. Five. Three.

They plunged into the welcoming darkness of the trees. Jack allowed himself a moment of relief – then realized with a spike of terror that he couldn't hear Marianne's gun anymore.

He turned, easing Tom down against a tree trunk. "Stay here," he ordered. "I'm going back for her."

Tom's hand shot out, gripping Jack's wrist with surprising strength. "Captain, you can't–"

But Jack was already moving, slipping back towards the edge of the orchard. He peered out, his heart in his throat.

Marianne was still there, using the doorway for cover. But she was pinned down, German fire keeping her from making a run for it. Even as Jack watched, her Sten clicked empty.

Without thinking, Jack burst from cover. "Marianne!" he shouted. "Come on!"

She looked up, surprise and something else – relief? fear? – flashing across her face. Then she was running, sprinting across the open ground with reckless abandon.

Jack provided covering fire, his pistol barking in the night. He wasn't aiming to hit, just to keep the Germans' heads down for a few crucial seconds.

It worked. Marianne reached him, breathing hard. "I told you to go," she gasped.

"Yeah, well, I've never been great at following orders," Jack replied. "Come on, we need to move."

They retreated into the orchard, using the trees for cover as they made their way back to Tom. The sergeant had managed to pull himself to his feet, leaning heavily against a gnarled trunk.

"Quite the rescue party, Captain," he said weakly. "Reminds me of Palermo. Remember that?"

Jack managed a grim chuckle. "Let's hope this one ends better. Can you make it a little further? We've got a rendezvous point about a kilometer from here."

Tom nodded, his jaw set with determination. "Lead the way, sir."

They set off through the orchard, moving as quickly and quietly as they could manage. Behind them, they could hear the sounds of pursuit – dogs barking, voices shouting in German. But the trees provided good cover, and soon the sounds began to fade into the distance.

After what felt like hours but was probably only twenty minutes, they reached a small clearing. Eduard and Marcel were there, looking tense but unharmed.

"Thank God," Eduard breathed as they emerged from the trees. "We were about to come looking for you."

"No time for reunions," Jack said tersely. "We need to move. The Germans won't be far behind."

Marcel nodded, already moving to help support Tom. "The truck is this way. We should be able to make it back to the vineyard before dawn."

As they made their way through the darkness, Jack felt the adrenaline beginning to ebb. In its wake came pain – his ankle throbbing in time with his heartbeat – and a bone-deep weariness. But underlying it all was a fierce sense of accomplishment. Against all odds, they'd done it. They'd rescued Tom.

He glanced at Marianne, walking beside him. Her face was streaked with dirt and sweat, her hair wild. But her eyes, when they met his, were shining with a fierce joy.

"We did it," she said softly, as if reading his thoughts.

Jack nodded, allowing himself a small smile. "Yeah. We did."

They reached the truck without incident. As Marcel and Eduard helped Tom into the back, Marianne turned to Jack.

"Jack, I–" she began, then stopped, seeming to struggle for words.

"What is it?" he prompted gently.

She met his eyes, and in that moment, all the unspoken things between them seemed to hang in the air. "Thank you," she said finally. "For coming back for me. You didn't have to do that."

Jack reached out, taking her hand in his. "Yes," he said quietly. "I did."

For a long moment, they stood like that, connected by touch and shared experience. Then Eduard's voice broke the spell.

"We need to go," he called softly. "It's not safe to linger."

Reality came crashing back. Jack gave Marianne's hand a final squeeze, then released it. "Let's go home," he said.

As they climbed into the truck, the first faint light of dawn was beginning to streak the eastern sky. Jack leaned back, feeling the vehicle rumble to life beneath him. They weren't out of danger yet – far from it. But they'd achieved the impossible. They'd successfully rescued one of their own from Nazi captivity and escaped, dealing a blow to local German operations.

ᗊᗊᗊ

7
Fleeting Silhouettes

The night air was thick with the scent of ripening grapes as Jack Holloway crouched at the edge of the vineyard. Beside him, Marianne Dupont peered through a pair of battered binoculars, her brow furrowed in concentration. In the valley below, the lights of the small town of Saint-Clair winked like earthbound stars.

"Anything?" Jack whispered, his hand unconsciously brushing the grip of his pistol.

Marianne shook her head, lowering the binoculars. "Nothing unusual. The usual patrols, but no sign of increased activity. It seems our little raid hasn't raised as many alarms as we feared."

Jack nodded, allowing himself a small sigh of relief. It had been three days since their daring rescue of Sergeant Tom O'Brien from the Nazi-held château. Three days of tense waiting, expecting at any moment to hear the rumble of German trucks coming to root them out. But so far, their luck had held.

"We should head back," Marianne said, her voice low. "Papa will be worried if we're gone too long."

As they rose to leave, a flicker of movement in the town below caught Jack's eye. He laid a hand on Marianne's arm, gesturing for silence. Peering into the darkness, he could just make out a convoy of vehicles entering the town square. Not the usual patrol jeeps, but larger trucks, canvas-covered and ominous in the moonlight.

"Well, well," Jack murmured. "What have we here?"

Marianne followed his gaze, her eyes narrowing. "That's not normal. The Germans never bring heavy vehicles into town at night. Too afraid of Resistance attacks."

Jack's mind raced, considering the implications. "Something big is happening. We need to get a closer look."

Marianne turned to him, her expression a mix of excitement and apprehension. "You can't be serious. It's too dangerous. If we're caught—"

"We won't be," Jack said with more confidence than he felt. "Come on, where's that famous French daring I've heard so much about?"

A smile tugged at the corners of Marianne's mouth. "Very well, Monsieur American. Lead the way. But if we end up in a German prison, I'm blaming you."

They made their way down the hillside, using the cover of olive groves and shadowy ravines. Jack's ankle, still not fully healed from his parachute landing, protested with each step. But the thrill of the mission, the potential importance of what they might discover, pushed the pain to the background.

As they neared the outskirts of Saint-Clair, the sound of voices carried on the night air. German voices, tense and urgent. Jack and Marianne exchanged a glance, then crept forward, using the deep shadows of an abandoned barn for cover.

The convoy had stopped in the town square, disgorging a stream of soldiers and... something else. Jack squinted, trying to make sense of what he was seeing. Men in civilian clothes, but moving with military precision. And with them, crates. Heavy wooden crates being unloaded with great care.

"What do you make of that?" he whispered to Marianne.

She shook her head, her expression troubled. "I'm not sure. But those men... they're not regular Wehrmacht. See how they move? The way they're dressed? I'd bet my last bottle of '36 Bordeaux they're SS."

Jack felt a chill run down his spine. The SS being involved changed everything. This wasn't just some routine military operation. Whatever was happening here was important. Dangerous.

A sharp cry split the night, followed by the sound of breaking glass. Jack tensed, his hand going to his weapon. But it was just a drunk, stumbling out of one of the few cafes still open at this hour. The man weaved his way across the square, singing an off-key rendition of "La Marseillaise."

The reaction from the Germans was immediate and brutal. Two soldiers broke from the group, converging on the drunk with ruthless efficiency. In seconds, they had him on the ground, a boot pressed to his neck.

Marianne made a small, pained sound. Jack laid a comforting hand on her arm, even as his own anger burned hot in his chest. They couldn't intervene, not without compromising their position. But the casual cruelty of it, the stark reminder of the occupation's reality, made his blood boil.

An officer — SS, Jack noted with grim certainty — strode over to the prone man. He said something too low to hear, then made a curt gesture. The soldiers hauled the drunk to his feet and dragged him towards one of the trucks.

"We have to do something," Marianne whispered urgently. "They'll kill him."

Jack's mind raced, weighing options, risks, potential outcomes. It went against every instinct to let an innocent civilian be taken. But revealing themselves now could jeopardize not just their lives, but the entire Resistance cell.

Before he could respond, a new sound cut through the night — the low, powerful thrum of approaching aircraft engines.

Every head in the square snapped skyward. For a moment, a wild hope surged in Jack's chest. Allied planes? A surprise raid?

But no. These aircraft were flying low and slow, their running lights clearly visible. As they passed overhead, Jack could make out the distinctive silhouettes of German transport planes. Junkers 52s, if he wasn't mistaken.

The SS officer barked orders, and the activity in the square redoubled. Whatever was in those crates, they were clearly in a hurry to get it loaded onto the planes.

"We need to get word back to Eduard," Jack said quietly. "This is big, Marianne. Whatever they're moving, it's important enough to risk night flights. If we can get that intel back to London—"

A sudden commotion from the square cut him off. The drunk, apparently finding a reserve of either courage or foolishness, had begun to struggle. As Jack and Marianne watched in horror, he broke free from his captors, stumbling directly towards their hiding place.

Time seemed to slow. Jack saw the glint of moonlight on gun barrels as the German soldiers raised their weapons. He saw the fear and determination on the drunk's face as he ran. And he saw the moment the man's bleary eyes locked onto their hiding spot.

In that instant, Jack knew they had a choice to make. A terrible, impossible choice.

If they revealed themselves, tried to help the man, they'd be captured or killed. The intelligence they'd gathered — potentially crucial information that could save countless lives — would be lost.

But if they stayed hidden, they'd be condemning an innocent man to death. A man whose only crime was a moment of drunken defiance against his oppressors.

Jack felt Marianne tense beside him, knew she was wrestling with the same awful calculus. He turned to her, saw the conflict raging in her eyes. In that moment, he realized that whatever decision they made, they'd make it together.

The drunk was mere meters away now. Behind him, Jack could hear the shouts of the pursuing soldiers, the ominous click of weapons being readied.

He met Marianne's gaze one last time. No words were needed. In her eyes, he saw the same mix of resolve and regret that he knew must be reflected in his own.

Together, they stepped out of the shadows.

What happened next was a blur of motion and sound. Jack's pistol barked twice, dropping the two nearest soldiers. Marianne's Sten gun chattered, laying down suppressing fire that sent the Germans diving for cover.

"Come on!" Jack shouted to the stunned drunk, grabbing his arm and hauling him towards the relative safety of a narrow alley.

They ran, the angry shouts of the Germans and the sporadic crack of gunfire spurring them on. Jack's ankle screamed in protest, but he pushed through the pain, one hand keeping a firm grip on the drunk's arm, the other returning fire whenever he could.

Marianne brought up the rear, her Sten gun's distinctive report covering their retreat. As they rounded a corner, Jack heard her cry out. He turned, heart in his throat, to see her stumble, one hand pressed to her side.

"I'm alright," she gasped, seeing his expression. "Just grazed. Keep moving!"

They plunged deeper into the maze of Saint-Clair's old town, the sounds of pursuit growing fainter. The drunk, sobered by fear and adrenaline, managed to keep pace. As they paused in the shadow of an old church to catch their breath, he turned to them with wide, disbelieving eyes.

"Who... who are you?" he stammered.

Jack and Marianne exchanged a glance. "Friends," Jack said simply. "Now, unless you want to spend the rest of the war in a German prison camp, I suggest you find somewhere to lay low for a while. Understand?"

The man nodded vigorously, then melted away into the night without another word.

"Well," Marianne said, wincing as she probed her injury, "I'd say that concludes our moonlit reconnaissance, wouldn't you?"

Despite the gravity of their situation, Jack couldn't help but chuckle. "I don't know. I think we've still got a few hours till dawn. Plenty of time to stir up more trouble."

Marianne's answering smile was equal parts exasperation and fondness. "You Americans. Always looking for the next fight."

The moment of levity passed quickly. They both knew the danger was far from over. The Germans would be on high alert now, and they still had to make it back to the relative safety of the vineyard.

"How bad is it?" Jack asked, nodding towards Marianne's wound.

She shook her head. "It's nothing. I've had worse from pruning the vines." But the tightness around her eyes belied her casual tone.

Jack made a decision. "Alright, change of plans. There's no way we're making it back to the vineyard tonight. We need to find a place to hole up, tend to that wound, and wait for things to calm down."

Marianne bit her lip, considering. Then she nodded. "I know a place. Old Madame Rousseau's house. She was... a friend of the Resistance. Died last winter, and no one's moved in since. It's not far."

They made their way through the darkened streets, every shadow seeming to hold potential danger. But luck, it seemed, was with them. They reached the small, shuttered house without incident.

Inside, the air was musty with disuse. Faded photographs on the walls hinted at a life long past — children grown, a husband lost to an earlier war. Jack felt a pang of melancholy, wondering what Old Madame Rousseau would think of her home being used as a hideout for fugitives.

He pushed the thought aside, focusing on the immediate needs. "Sit," he ordered Marianne, guiding her to a dusty armchair. "Let me take a look at that wound."

As he tended to her injury — which was, thankfully, little more than a deep graze — Jack's mind whirled with the implications of what they'd seen. The SS presence, the mysterious crates, the night flights... Something big was happening. Something that could potentially change the course of the war.

"We need to get this information back to Eduard," he said as he finished bandaging Marianne's side. "And from there to London. Whatever the Germans are up to, it can't be good."

Marianne nodded, her face pale in the dim light filtering through the shuttered windows. "Agreed. But Jack... what we did tonight. Revealing ourselves, risking everything for one man..."

She trailed off, but Jack understood the unspoken question. Had it been worth it? Had they jeopardized their entire mission, potentially crucial intelligence, for the sake of a single, unknown drunk?

"We did what we had to do," Jack said quietly. "What we could live with. Sometimes... sometimes that's all we can do in this war. Make the choices we can live with."

Marianne was silent for a long moment. Then she reached out, taking Jack's hand in hers. "Thank you," she said softly. "For understanding. For... being here."

Jack felt a warmth spread through him that had nothing to do with the adrenaline of their escape. He squeezed her hand gently. "Always," he replied.

As the first light of dawn began to seep through the cracks in the shutters, Jack and Marianne sat in companionable silence. Both lost in thought, both acutely aware of the challenges that lay ahead. But also, in some indefinable way, stronger for having faced this night together.

The moonlit reconnaissance had yielded more than just military intelligence. It had forged a bond, a partnership, that Jack sensed would be tested in the days to come. But looking at Marianne, seeing the quiet strength in her eyes, he felt a surge of something he hadn't dared feel in a long time.

Hope.

❥❥❥

69

8
Smoke and Ashes

The pre-dawn mist clung to the vineyards of Château Espérance like a shroud, muffling sound and obscuring vision. Jack Holloway and Marianne Dupont moved through it like ghosts, their footsteps silent on the dew-dampened earth. They had left their hiding place in Saint-Clair as soon as the curfew lifted, eager to return to the relative safety of the vineyard and share their crucial intelligence.

As they neared the château, Jack felt a prickle of unease. Something was off. The air was too still, the silence too complete. No birdsong, no distant sounds of work beginning in the fields. Just... nothing.

He caught Marianne's eye, saw his own concern mirrored there. Without a word, they both slowed their pace, hands drifting to their weapons.

They rounded the final bend in the path, and Jack's heart sank. The courtyard of Château Espérance was filled with German vehicles. Soldiers milled about, their feldgrau uniforms a stark contrast to the ancient stones and verdant vines.

"Merde," Marianne breathed, her face pale with shock and fear.

Jack's mind raced. Had they been compromised? Was this a raid, or something else? And what of Eduard, Marcel, and the others?

Before he could voice any of these questions, a figure emerged from the main house. Even at this distance, Jack recognized the imperious bearing of an SS officer. His stomach clenched as he realized it was the same man they had seen coordinating the mysterious nighttime activities in Saint-Clair.

The officer was not alone. Eduard Dupont walked beside him, his face a mask of careful neutrality. They seemed to be deep in conversation, Eduard gesturing occasionally towards the vineyards.

"What the hell?" Jack muttered, thoroughly confused now.

Marianne grabbed his arm, her grip painfully tight. "We need to get out of here," she hissed. "Now."

But it was too late. One of the German soldiers had spotted them. He raised his rifle, barking out a challenge in guttural German.

Jack's hand went to his pistol, but Marianne stopped him with a sharp shake of her head. "No," she said, her voice tight with some emotion Jack couldn't quite identify. "We surrender."

Before Jack could protest, she was stepping forward, hands raised. "Ne tirez pas!" she called out. "Don't shoot! We live here!"

The next few minutes passed in a blur. They were surrounded, disarmed, roughly searched. Jack's mind whirled, trying to make sense of what was happening. Why had Marianne given up so easily? What game was Eduard playing, chatting amiably with an SS officer while his home was occupied?

They were marched into the courtyard, where Eduard and the SS officer turned to regard them. Jack searched his friend's face for some sign, some clue as to what was going on. But Eduard's expression remained impassive, revealing nothing.

"Ah, Marianne," the SS officer said, his French impeccable but colored with a distinct German accent. "How kind of you to join us. Your father and I were just discussing the excellent vintages produced by your family's vineyard."

Marianne's face was a study in conflicting emotions – fear, confusion, and something else. Something that looked unsettlingly like guilt. "Herr Sturmbannführer," she said, her voice carefully neutral. "I wasn't aware we were expecting... guests."

The officer smiled, a cold expression that didn't reach his eyes. "Oh, come now. Surely your father mentioned our arrangement? After all, it's been in place for... how long has it been, Monsieur Dupont?"

"Six months, Sturmbannführer Richter," Eduard replied, his voice steady but devoid of its usual warmth.

Jack felt as though the ground had dropped out from beneath him. Six months. The Duponts had been collaborating with the Nazis for six months. Which meant...

"You son of a bitch," he growled, lunging towards Eduard. Strong hands grabbed him, held him back. "All this time, you've been playing us! The Resistance, the rescue mission – it was all a lie!"

Eduard flinched at the accusation, real pain flashing across his face. But before he could respond, Sturmbannführer Richter stepped forward, his cold smile widening.

"Ah yes, the American," he said, switching to lightly accented English. "Captain Jack Holloway, if I'm not mistaken. We've been quite interested in you and your little band of saboteurs."

Jack said nothing, glaring at the SS officer with undisguised hatred. His mind raced, trying to piece together the full extent of the betrayal. How much did the Germans know? What had happened to Mike, to the other members of the Resistance cell?

As if reading his thoughts, Richter continued. "Oh, don't worry about your compatriots. They're quite safe. For now." His tone hardened. "Their continued well-being, however, depends entirely on your cooperation."

"Go to hell," Jack spat.

Richter's smile didn't waver. "Come now, Captain. Let's dispense with the tedious bravado. You're an intelligent man. Surely you can see the futility of your situation." He began to pace, hands clasped behind his back. "The war is lost for you, you must realize that. Germany's victory is inevitable. The only question is how much more blood must be spilled before the Allies accept the new order."

Jack said nothing, his jaw clenched so tight it ached. Richter continued, warming to his subject.

"But it doesn't have to end in more senseless death. You have skills, Captain. Knowledge. Things that could be of great use to the Reich. Help us, and you'll be treated well. You have my word as an officer."

"The word of a Nazi isn't worth much," Jack growled.

Richter's eyes hardened. "Perhaps not to you. But surely the word of your... friends... holds more weight?"

He gestured, and Eduard stepped forward. The older man's face was lined with tension and what looked unsettlingly like shame. "Jack," he said softly. "Please. Listen to them. It's the only way."

Jack stared at Eduard in disbelief. This was the man who had welcomed him into his home, who had fought alongside him, who had spoken so passionately of resisting tyranny. And now...

"Why?" he asked, unable to keep the hurt and betrayal from his voice.

Eduard's shoulders slumped. "You don't understand. None of you do. This land, this vineyard – it's been in my family for generations. When the Germans came, they were going to take it all. Destroy everything we've built. I couldn't... I couldn't let that happen."

"So you sold out your country instead?" Jack's voice dripped with contempt.

"I made a choice!" Eduard snapped, real anger flashing in his eyes. "A choice to protect what matters most. You think it was easy? You think I don't lie awake every night, hating myself for what I've done? But I did what I had to do to survive. To ensure that when this madness is over, there's still something left to rebuild from."

Jack shook his head, disgusted. "There are some things more important than survival."

"Easy for you to say," Marianne cut in, her voice tight with emotion. "You're not the one who has to live with the consequences. This is our home, Jack. Our life. You... you're just passing through."

The words hit Jack like a physical blow. He turned to Marianne, searching her face for some sign that this was all an act, some clever ruse. But all he saw was a mixture of defiance and shame.

"Et tu, Brute?" he murmured, the fight suddenly going out of him.

Richter clapped his hands, looking pleased. "Well! I'm glad we're all beginning to see reason. Now, Captain Holloway, why don't we continue this discussion somewhere more comfortable? I'm sure once you've had some time to consider your position, you'll make the right choice."

As the German soldiers moved to lead him away, Jack's gaze locked with Marianne's one last time. In her eyes, he saw a whirlpool of conflicting emotions – regret, fear, and something else. Something that looked almost like... hope?

Before he could puzzle out what it meant, he was being marched towards the château. As he crossed the threshold, the heavy wooden door closing behind him with a sense of finality, Jack couldn't shake the feeling that he was leaving more than just his freedom behind.

Inside, the familiar warmth of Château Espérance had been replaced by a cold, military efficiency. Maps and radio equipment cluttered the once-homey sitting room. German soldiers moved about with purposeful strides, barely sparing Jack a glance as he was led past.

Richter ushered him into Eduard's study, now transformed into an impromptu interrogation room. As Jack was forced into a chair, his hands cuffed behind him, he took in the changes with a sense of surreal detachment. The shelf that had once held prized vintages now displayed a row of neatly labeled files. Eduard's beloved antique desk was covered in official-looking documents bearing the eagle and swastika of the Third Reich.

"Comfortable?" Richter asked, seating himself across from Jack with infuriating casualness.

Jack said nothing, fixing the SS officer with a glare of pure loathing.

Richter sighed theatrically. "Come now, Captain. There's no need for this silent treatment. We're all civilized men here. Well," he amended with a cold smile, "some of us more than others."

When Jack still didn't respond, Richter's expression hardened. "Very well. If you insist on being difficult, perhaps a demonstration of the consequences is in order."

He snapped his fingers, and a soldier entered, dragging a battered and bloodied figure. Jack's heart sank as he recognized Marcel, the fiery young Resistance fighter. The man's face was a mass of bruises, one eye swollen shut. But as he raised his head and saw Jack, a flicker of defiance crossed his features.

"You see, Captain," Richter said conversationally, "your friend here has been most uncooperative. Admirably loyal, I must say. But loyalty can be... inconvenient."

He nodded to the soldier, who drove a vicious punch into Marcel's midsection. The young man doubled over, gasping for air.

"Stop," Jack growled, unable to watch the brutality any longer.

Richter raised an eyebrow. "Oh? Have we found your weakness, Captain? How disappointing. I had such high hopes for your American resolve."

Jack's mind raced, searching for a way out of this impossible situation. He couldn't give the Nazis what they wanted – that much was certain. But neither could he stand by and watch them torture Marcel, or any of the others.

"What do you want?" he asked finally, hating the defeat in his voice.

Richter smiled, the expression of a predator that knows its prey is cornered. "Information, Captain. About your mission, your contacts, the full extent of Allied operations in this region. You give me that, and I give you my word that your friends will be treated humanely."

Jack's eyes narrowed. "And if I don't?"

The SS officer's smile turned cruel. "Then I'm afraid Monsieur Marcel here will be only the first to suffer for your stubbornness. I wonder... how long do you think the lovely Mademoiselle Dupont will last under questioning?"

A red haze of fury clouded Jack's vision. He lunged forward, forgetting for a moment that he was restrained. "You touch her, and I swear to God I'll–"

"You'll what?" Richter cut him off, amused. "Face it, Captain. You've lost. The only question now is how many people will suffer before you accept that fact."

Jack slumped back in his chair, the fight draining out of him. He glanced at Marcel, saw the mixture of pain and determination in the young man's eyes. What would Tom do in this situation? Or Mike? What was the right call when there were no good options left?

As he wrestled with the impossible choice before him, a commotion erupted outside the study. Shouts in German, the sound of running feet. Richter frowned, rising from his chair.

"What now?" he muttered, moving to the door.

Before he could reach it, the door burst open. A breathless German soldier stumbled in, his eyes wide with panic. "Herr Sturmbannführer!" he gasped. "The vineyard – it's on fire!"

Richter's composure cracked for the first time. "Was? Impossible! How could–"

His words were cut off by a deafening explosion that shook the very foundations of the château. In the chaos that followed, Jack's training kicked in. He threw himself sideways, toppling his chair and using the momentum to roll behind the heavy oak desk.

As German shouts and the crackle of flames filled the air, Jack allowed himself a grim smile. It seemed the seeds of resistance had taken root after all. Whatever happened next, he knew one thing for certain – this fight was far from over.

᠉᠉᠉

9

A Soldier's Gamble

Chaos reigned in the study of Château Espérance. Smoke billowed through the shattered windows, acrid and thick. The sounds of gunfire and shouting echoed from the courtyard. Jack Holloway, still handcuffed and crouched behind the heavy oak desk, felt his heart pounding in his chest. This was his chance – perhaps his only chance.

Sturmbannführer Richter was shouting orders in rapid-fire German, his earlier composure completely shattered. The soldier who had burst in with news of the fire lay crumpled by the door, felled by falling debris from the explosion. And Marcel...

Jack's eyes widened as he saw the young Resistance fighter moving with surprising speed for someone so battered. In the confusion, Marcel had managed to get his hands on a letter opener from the desk. As Jack watched, he drove the improvised weapon into the back of Richter's thigh.

The SS officer went down with a howl of pain and rage. Marcel wasted no time, diving for the fallen soldier's sidearm. But he was slowed by his injuries, and Richter, despite the blade protruding from his leg, was faster.

The gun went off with a deafening crack in the enclosed space. Marcel stumbled backward, a look of surprise on his face as a crimson stain blossomed on his shirt.

"No!" Jack shouted, surging to his feet. But there was nothing he could do, hands still bound behind him, as Marcel crumpled to the floor.

Richter turned, his face a mask of pain and fury, the gun now trained on Jack. "You," he snarled. "This is your doing somehow. I don't know how, but–"

His words were cut off as the door burst open once more. Jack tensed, expecting more German soldiers. Instead, a familiar voice rang out.

"Drop the gun, Nazi bastard, or I'll ventilate that thick skull of yours."

Lieutenant Mike Carpenter stood in the doorway, battered and pale but very much alive. In his hands, he held Richter's own Luger, liberated from the desk during the chaos.

Richter's eyes darted between Mike and Jack, calculation warring with rage on his face. For a moment, Jack thought he might try to shoot anyway. But then, with a grimace of pain and frustration, the SS officer lowered his weapon.

"Mike," Jack breathed, relief washing over him. "Boy, am I glad to see you."

"Likewise, Captain," Mike said, not taking his eyes off Richter. "Though I gotta say, you look like hell."

"You should see the other guy," Jack quipped, nodding towards Richter.

Mike's expression hardened as he took in the scene – the fallen Marcel, the letter opener still protruding from Richter's leg. "Oh, I intend to," he said grimly.

Before anyone could react further, another explosion rocked the château. The already damaged window frame gave way entirely, showering the room with glass and debris.

"Much as I'd love to stay and chat," Mike said, "I think that's our cue to leave. You okay to move, Jack?"

Jack nodded, already heading for the door. "Just get these cuffs off me and point me towards a weapon. I've got a score to settle."

As Mike worked on the handcuffs, Jack's mind raced. "The others?" he asked urgently. "Tom? Eduard? Marianne?"

A shadow passed over Mike's face. "Tom's safe. We got him out when the shooting started. Eduard..." He trailed off, something like disgust in his voice. "Let's just say the old man's got a lot of explaining to do. As for Marianne, last I saw she was giving the Germans hell in the courtyard. Girl's got a mean right hook."

Jack felt a surge of conflicting emotions at the mention of Marianne. Relief that she was alive and fighting, confusion over her apparent betrayal, and something else... something he wasn't quite ready to name.

The cuffs finally fell away, and Jack flexed his wrists gratefully. Mike handed him Richter's Luger, keeping the fallen soldier's sidearm for himself. "What about him?" Jack asked, jerking his head towards the now-unconscious SS officer.

Mike's expression turned grim. "Much as I'd like to put a bullet in his brain, we might need him. Intel, bargaining chip... who knows."

Jack nodded reluctantly. As much as he hated to admit it, Mike was right. "Alright. Let's truss him up and take him with us. But first..."

He knelt beside Marcel, checking for a pulse with a sinking heart. To his amazement, he found one – weak and thready, but there. "He's alive," Jack said, a note of wonder in his voice. "Tough son of a bitch."

"Must be something in the wine around here," Mike quipped, already moving to help Jack with Marcel. "Come on, let's get them both out of here before this whole place comes down around our ears."

They worked quickly, field-dressing Marcel's wound as best they could and securing Richter with his own belt and Jack's discarded handcuffs. As they maneuvered their burdens towards the door, Jack couldn't help but ask, "Mike... what the hell happened out there? Last I knew, you were laid up with broken ribs, and the Germans had us all but beaten."

Mike grinned, a fierce light in his eyes despite his obvious exhaustion. "Funny story, that. Turns out our friends in the Resistance had an ace up their sleeve. Or should I say, a few dozen aces, all armed to the teeth and mad as hell at the Nazis."

Jack's eyebrows shot up. "You're kidding. The Maquis?"

"The very same," Mike confirmed as they started down the smoke-filled hallway. "Guess Eduard and Marianne's little double-agent act paid off after all."

Jack nearly stumbled in surprise. "Double-agent? You mean..."

"Yeah," Mike said, his tone a mixture of admiration and exasperation. "Seems the Duponts have been playing a long game. Feeding the Germans just enough intel to stay in their good graces, all while setting up this little surprise party. Gotta hand it to them – they had me fooled too."

Jack's mind reeled with the implications. The betrayal, the collaboration – it had all been an act? Part of him felt a surge of relief and admiration. But another part, a part he wasn't proud of, felt a stab of hurt. Why hadn't they trusted him with the truth?

There was no time to dwell on it, though. As they emerged into the courtyard, Jack was met with a scene of controlled chaos. Men in civilian clothes – the Maquis, he assumed – were engaged in fierce firefights with the remaining German soldiers. The air was thick with gunsmoke and the acrid scent of burning vines.

And there, in the thick of it all, was Marianne. She moved with deadly grace, her Sten gun chattering as she provided covering fire for a group of Maquis fighters advancing on a German position. Her face was smudged with soot, her hair wild, but to Jack, she had never looked more beautiful – or more dangerous.

Their eyes met across the battlefield, and for a moment, the world seemed to fade away. Jack saw relief in her gaze, and something else... something that made his heart race in a way that had nothing to do with the danger around them.

The moment was shattered by a shout from nearby. "Capitaine! Par ici!"

Jack turned to see a grizzled man in his fifties waving them towards a battered truck. His weather-beaten face split in a fierce grin as they approached. "Ah, les Américains! Always making a grand entrance, non? Come, we must go. The Germans, they are bringing reinforcements."

As they loaded Marcel and the still-unconscious Richter into the truck, Jack caught sight of Eduard. The older man was coordinating the Maquis' retreat, his earlier facade of collaboration replaced by the unmistakable bearing of a resistance leader.

Their eyes met, and Eduard gave him a nod – part apology, part salute. Jack returned it, a wordless acknowledgment passing between them. There would be time for explanations later. For now, survival was all that mattered.

The truck's engine roared to life, and they began to pull away from the burning château. Jack felt a pang of something – regret? nostalgia? – as he watched the place that had been his home for the past weeks recede into the distance. So much had happened there, so much had changed. He wondered if he'd ever see it again.

As if reading his thoughts, Marianne appeared at his side. She was breathing hard, her face flushed with exertion and what might have been embarrassment. "Jack," she began, "I–"

He cut her off with a raised hand. "Later," he said, not unkindly. "We've got more pressing concerns right now."

She nodded, understanding in her eyes. But as she turned to go, Jack caught her arm. "Marianne," he said softly. "I'm glad you're okay."

A small smile tugged at the corners of her mouth. "You too, mon capitaine," she replied. Then she was gone, moving to help tend to Marcel's wounds.

As the truck bounced along the rutted country roads, putting distance between them and the chaos they'd left behind, Jack allowed himself a moment to take stock. They had suffered losses, yes. The vineyard was likely destroyed, their safe haven compromised. Marcel was gravely wounded, and they were now burdened with a high-ranking Nazi prisoner.

But they were alive. They had struck a significant blow against the German occupation. And perhaps most importantly, they had tasted freedom – real, hard-won freedom – for the first time in what felt like an eternity.

Jack's musings were interrupted by Mike, who settled beside him with a groan. "So," the lieutenant said conversationally, "I don't suppose you have any idea where we're going?"

Jack shook his head, a wry smile tugging at his lips. "Not a clue. But you know what, Mike? For the first time since we landed in this godforsaken country, I'm actually looking forward to finding out."

Mike chuckled, then winced as the movement jarred his still-healing ribs. "You always did have a weird definition of fun, boss."

The truck crested a hill, revealing a panoramic view of the valley below. In the distance, Jack could see the faint outlines of a small village nestled among rolling hills. It looked peaceful, untouched by the war that raged around it.

"Bienvenue à La Résistance," the grizzled Maquis leader called out from the driver's seat. "Welcome to the heart of the French Resistance."

As they descended into the valley, Jack felt a sense of anticipation building in his chest. This was it – the real fight was just beginning. And for the first time in a long while, he felt truly ready for it.

The taste of freedom, he realized, was addictive. And he was hungry for more.

ϷϷϷ

10
Under the Red Cross

The village of Saint-Clair-sur-Epte nestled in the valley like a secret, its ancient stone buildings a patchwork of sun-bleached tiles and weathered timber. As the battered truck carrying Jack and his companions rumbled down the narrow main street, curious faces peered out from behind half-drawn curtains.

Jack felt the weight of those unseen gazes, a mixture of hope and wariness that seemed to characterize life in occupied France. He shifted uncomfortably in his seat, acutely aware of his disheveled appearance and the dried blood – some his, some not – that stained his borrowed clothes.

The truck came to a stop in front of a modest stone building with a faded red cross painted above the door. "L'hôpital," the grizzled Maquis leader, who had introduced himself as Henri, announced. "Not much, but the best we have for your wounded."

As if on cue, Marcel let out a low groan from where he lay in the back of the truck. The young resistance fighter had been slipping in and out of consciousness during the journey, his face pale and drawn with pain.

"Let's get him inside," Jack said, already moving to help. "Mike, you too. I want those ribs looked at properly."

Mike opened his mouth as if to protest, but a sharp look from Jack silenced him. "Yes, sir," he muttered, climbing gingerly from the truck.

As they maneuvered Marcel's limp form towards the hospital entrance, Jack caught sight of Marianne speaking urgently with her father. Eduard's face was grave as he listened, nodding occasionally. Whatever they were discussing, it was clear the weight of recent events sat heavily on both their shoulders.

Inside, the hospital was a far cry from the sterile, well-equipped facilities Jack was used to. The main room was lined with simple cots, most occupied by men bearing the obvious signs of combat. The air was thick with the smell of antiseptic and something else – fear, pain, the lingering specter of death.

A harried-looking woman in a nurse's uniform approached them, her eyes widening as she took in Marcel's condition. "Par ici," she said briskly, gesturing towards an empty cot. "Vite!"

As they settled Marcel onto the cot, Jack stepped back, suddenly feeling very out of place. This was a world beyond his expertise – the delicate art of putting broken bodies back together. He was more accustomed to the breaking.

A hand on his arm startled him from his thoughts. He turned to find Marianne at his side, her face etched with concern. "Jack," she said softly. "You should let someone look at you as well. You're injured."

He blinked, surprised. In the chaos of their escape, he'd almost forgotten about his own injuries – the dull throb in his ankle, the various cuts and bruises that mapped the events of the past few days across his skin.

"I'm fine," he started to say, but Marianne was already steering him towards another cot.

"You're not fine," she said firmly. "And we need you at your best. Please, Jack. Let me help."

There was something in her voice, a note of... what? Guilt? Pleading? Whatever it was, Jack found he didn't have the energy to argue. He sank onto the cot with a sigh, the events of the past days suddenly crashing over him in a wave of bone-deep exhaustion.

Marianne's hands were gentle as she began to clean and dress his wounds. Jack watched her work, struck by the competence and care in her movements.

"Where did you learn to do this?" he asked, wincing slightly as she dabbed antiseptic on a particularly nasty cut on his forearm.

A small, sad smile tugged at her lips. "My mother," she said softly. "She was a nurse in the Great War. She always said that in times of conflict, healing hands were as important as fighting ones."

Jack nodded, understanding. "She sounds like a wise woman."

"She was," Marianne replied, her voice thick with emotion. Then, almost too quietly for Jack to hear, she added, "I hope she would be proud of what we're doing."

The vulnerability in her tone stirred something in Jack's chest. Without thinking, he reached out, covering her hand with his own. "I'm sure she would be," he said softly.

Marianne looked up, her eyes meeting his. For a long moment, they stayed like that, connected by touch and unspoken understanding. Then, with visible effort, Marianne pulled away, returning her attention to Jack's injuries.

"I owe you an explanation," she said as she worked, her voice low and intense. "About what happened at the château. About... everything."

Jack tensed, the hurt and confusion of the apparent betrayal rushing back. But he forced himself to remain calm, to listen. "I'm all ears," he said, keeping his tone neutral.

Marianne took a deep breath, her hands stilling for a moment. "It started long before you arrived," she began. "When the Germans first came, they... they were going to take everything. The château, the vineyard, all of it. My father, he... he made a choice."

She paused, seeming to struggle with the weight of the memory. Jack remained silent, giving her the space to continue.

"He offered to collaborate," Marianne went on. "To provide information, to be their eyes and ears in the region. But it was all a ruse. From the very beginning, he was working with the Resistance. Feeding the Germans just enough truth to keep them satisfied, while using his position to gather real intelligence for the Allies."

Jack's mind raced, piecing together the implications. "The entire time I was there..."

Marianne nodded. "We were walking a tightrope. Every day, every interaction, was a careful dance of truth and deception. When you and your men arrived, it... complicated things."

"Because you couldn't be sure if we were who we said we were," Jack finished, understanding dawning.

"Exactly," Marianne said, relief evident in her voice. "We had to maintain the illusion, even with you, until we could be certain. And then, when we were... we couldn't risk breaking cover. The plan with the Maquis was already in motion. If we had told you..."

"I might have reacted in a way that gave the game away," Jack said, a rueful smile tugging at his lips. "I'm not exactly known for my poker face."

A ghost of a smile flickered across Marianne's face. "No, you're not," she agreed. Then her expression sobered. "Jack, I... we never wanted to hurt you. To betray your trust. But the stakes were so high. Can you understand that?"

Jack was silent for a long moment, turning it all over in his mind. The hurt was still there, a dull ache beneath his ribs. But mixed with it now was a growing admiration for the courage and resolve it must have taken to maintain such a dangerous charade.

"I understand," he said finally. "I don't like it. But I understand."

Marianne's shoulders sagged with relief. "Thank you," she said softly. Then, with a hint of her usual spirit, she added, "Though I have to say, your reaction in the château was quite convincing. For a moment, I thought you might actually believe we had turned traitor."

Jack chuckled, then winced as the movement pulled at his injuries. "Well, I've picked up a few acting skills of my own along the way. Though I have to admit, the genuine shock and outrage probably helped sell it."

Marianne's smile faded. "I'm sorry," she said again. "For all of it. For putting you in that position. For..."

She trailed off, her eyes dropping to where her hand still rested on his arm. Jack felt a surge of warmth that had nothing to do with his injuries.

"Hey," he said gently, waiting until she looked up at him. "We're okay. Alright? We're okay."

Marianne nodded, blinking rapidly against what might have been tears. Then, with visible effort, she pulled herself together, returning to the task of tending his wounds.

As she worked, Jack let his gaze wander around the makeshift hospital. He saw Mike, grimacing as a doctor examined his ribs. Eduard, deep in conversation with Henri and several other men who had to be Maquis leaders. And there, in a corner under heavy guard, the still-unconscious form of Sturmbannführer Richter.

"What are we going to do with him?" Jack asked, nodding towards the SS officer.

Marianne followed his gaze, her expression hardening. "That's for the Maquis leadership to decide. But if it were up to me..." She trailed off, but the steel in her voice left little doubt as to her preferred course of action.

Jack nodded, understanding. The brutality of war had a way of hardening even the gentlest souls. And Marianne, for all her compassion, was far from gentle when it came to the enemies of France.

"He could be valuable," Jack mused. "Intel, bargaining chip... assuming he can be made to talk."

A cold smile played at the corners of Marianne's mouth. "Oh, I think we can manage that. Marcel may be injured, but his skill with... persuasion... is undiminished."

Jack felt a chill at her words, a reminder that for all their shared moments of warmth and connection, there was still much about Marianne – about all of them – that remained in shadow.

Before he could respond, a commotion at the hospital entrance drew their attention. A group of Maquis fighters burst in, supporting between them a figure Jack recognized with a jolt of surprise.

"Tom?" he exclaimed, starting to rise. Marianne put a restraining hand on his shoulder.

"Easy," she cautioned. "Let them bring him to us."

Sergeant Tom O'Brien looked like he'd been through hell. His uniform was in tatters, his face a mass of cuts and bruises. But his eyes, when they met Jack's, were clear and alert.

"Fancy meeting you here, Captain," he quipped as the Maquis lowered him onto a nearby cot. "Looks like I missed quite a party."

Jack felt a grin spreading across his face despite the gravity of the situation. "You have no idea, Sergeant. But I'm damned glad to see you in one piece."

As Marianne moved to examine Tom's injuries, Jack filled him in on recent events – the raid on the château, the revelation of the Duponts' true allegiance, their narrow escape.

Tom listened intently, his expression a mixture of surprise and grudging admiration. "Well, I'll be damned," he said when Jack had finished. "And here I thought I was having an exciting time, playing hide and seek with Nazi patrols in the woods."

"Speaking of which," Jack said, his tone growing serious, "what happened out there, Tom? Last we knew, you were being held for interrogation."

A shadow passed over the sergeant's face. "It's a long story, Captain. And not a pretty one. But the short version is... I had help. From inside the German ranks."

Jack's eyebrows shot up. "A defector?"

Tom shook his head. "Not exactly. More like... a sympathizer. Someone who's been playing a similar game to our friends here." He nodded towards Marianne. "Feeding information to the Resistance, sabotaging operations where they can. They risked everything to get me out."

"Who?" Jack asked, leaning forward with interest.

Tom hesitated, glancing around the crowded hospital. "I think that's a conversation best had in private, sir. There are... complications."

Jack nodded, understanding. In the world they now inhabited, trust was a precious and fragile commodity. "Alright. We'll debrief fully once we're somewhere more secure. For now, just rest and recover. That's an order, Sergeant."

Tom managed a weak salute. "Yes, sir. Though I have to say, you look like you could use some rest yourself."

Jack chuckled, feeling the weight of exhaustion settling over him once more. "You're not wrong there."

As if on cue, Marianne reappeared at his side. "Both of you need rest," she said firmly. "Doctor's orders. Or nurse's orders, at least."

Jack opened his mouth to protest, but a stern look from Marianne silenced him. "Alright, alright," he conceded. "But wake me if anything changes. If Richter comes around, or if there's any news about Marcel's condition."

Marianne's expression softened. "Of course," she said. Then, more quietly, "Get some sleep, Jack. You're no good to anyone if you run yourself into the ground."

As Jack settled back onto the cot, he felt the accumulated tension of the past days begin to ebb. The hospital around him was a hive of quiet activity – whispered conversations, the soft footsteps of nurses, the occasional groan of pain quickly hushed.

But beneath it all was something else. A current of energy, of purpose. These people – the Maquis, the villagers who sheltered them, his own team – they were no longer just surviving. They were fighting back.

As sleep began to claim him, Jack's last coherent thought was of Marianne. Of the gentle strength in her hands as she tended his wounds, the fire in her eyes as she spoke of resistance. Whatever lay ahead, whatever challenges they would face, he knew one thing for certain.

ϷϷϷ

11

The Storm's Eye

"See anything?" Jack Holloway's whisper barely carried over the pre-dawn breeze.

Marianne Dupont lowered her battered binoculars, her breath forming small clouds in the cool air. "Right on schedule. Just like Marcel said."

"How many?"

"I count seven trucks. Snaking along like fireflies down there."

Jack's hand unconsciously checked his pistol. "Well, I'll be damned. Looks like our intel was good after all."

"Marcel's contact came through. Again." Marianne's tone held a note of grudging admiration. "For a collaborator, he's proving remarkably useful."

"Yeah, about that..." Jack shifted uneasily. "Don't you think it's a bit convenient? I mean, ever since we busted out of Château Espérance, Marcel's made this 'miraculous recovery' and suddenly we're swimming in high-quality intel."

Marianne turned to face him, her expression sharp in the dim light. "You think it's a trap?"

"I'm saying we can't rule it out. This source of his, buried deep in German ranks? We don't even know who it is."

"But every piece of information has checked out so far," Marianne countered. "Including this." She gestured towards the convoy below.

Jack sighed. "I know, I know. It's just... we're relying awfully heavily on information we can't verify."

"You're not wrong." Marianne's voice softened. "But Jack, this is too big an opportunity to pass up. If those trucks are carrying what we think they are..."

"Critical components for their new radar installation," Jack finished. "Yeah, I get it. The intelligence value alone would be huge, not to mention the blow to their operations."

"Exactly." Marianne placed a hand on his arm. "So, are we doing this or not?"

Jack met her gaze, seeing the determination there. After a moment, he nodded. "Alright. But let's go over the plan one more time. I want to make sure everyone's on the same page."

Marianne rolled her eyes, but there was a fond smile playing at the corners of her mouth. "Again? Very well, mon capitaine. Walk me through it."

The convoy will reach the ambush point in approximately twenty minutes. Henri and his team are in position here and here." She pointed to spots on a crude map scratched in the dirt. "They'll disable the lead and rear vehicles, bottlenecking the convoy in the ravine."

Jack picked up the thread. "Meanwhile, Tom and Mike will provide covering fire from these ridges, preventing any organized counterattack. That's when we move in with the main assault team. Quick and dirty – neutralize any resistance, secure the cargo, and exfil to the rendezvous point."

"And I," Marianne added, a hint of steel in her voice, "will be right beside you. Don't even think about trying to leave me behind this time."

Jack met her gaze, seeing the fierce determination there. He knew better than to argue. Besides, if he was honest with himself, he felt better knowing she'd be watching his back.

"Wouldn't dream of it," he said with a wry smile. Then, more seriously, "Just... be careful out there. Okay?"

Something softened in Marianne's eyes. "Always," she said softly. Then, with a quick squeeze of his hand, she was all business again. "We should move. The others will be waiting."

They made their way down the hillside, using the pre-dawn gloom and the cover of the dense forest to mask their approach. As they neared the ambush point, Jack could make out the shadowy forms of Resistance fighters taking up their positions. Henri's grizzled face appeared out of the darkness, nodding a terse greeting.

"All is ready," the Maquis leader reported in his heavily accented English. "We await only your signal, Capitaine."

Jack nodded, feeling the familiar tension coiling in his gut. This was the moment he both loved and hated – the calm before the storm, when all the planning and preparation came down to split-second decisions and the cruel vagaries of fate.

He turned to Marianne, seeing his own mix of anticipation and apprehension mirrored in her eyes. "Last chance to back out," he said, only half-joking.

She answered with a fierce grin. "And miss all the fun? Not a chance, American."

Before Jack could respond, the distant rumble of engines reached their ears. He held up a hand, signaling for silence. The atmosphere grew taut with expectation as the sound grew louder, punctuated by the creak of leather and the soft metallic clicks of weapons being readied.

The lead vehicle of the convoy came into view, its headlights cutting through the early morning mist. Jack counted under his breath. One... two... three...

"Now," he said quietly.

The word had barely left his lips when two explosions rocked the ravine. The lead and rear vehicles erupted in flames, their drivers caught completely off guard. Chaos erupted as German soldiers poured from the trapped trucks, shouting in confusion and fear.

"Go!" Jack barked, and the night came alive with gunfire.

He surged forward, Marianne a steady presence at his side. The world narrowed to a series of vivid, violent snapshots. The look of shock on a young German soldier's face as Jack's bullet found its mark. The staccato chatter of Marianne's Sten gun as she provided covering fire. The acrid smell of cordite mixing with the damp earth and burning fuel.

They fought their way to the central truck, where intelligence suggested the radar components were stored. Jack took down two guards with quick, efficient shots, then turned to cover Marianne as she worked on the lock.

"Hurry," he urged, aware that their window of opportunity was rapidly closing. Already, he could hear shouts of German reinforcements approaching from further down the road.

Marianne muttered something that sounded distinctly unflattering in French, then gave a cry of triumph as the lock gave way. "Got it!"

They clambered into the truck, quickly locating the crates they'd come for. Jack's heart raced as he pried one open, revealing a jumble of electronic components that meant little to him but would be worth their weight in gold to Allied intelligence.

"Jackpot," he breathed.

A shout from outside snapped him back to the present danger. "Time to go," he said, already moving to grab one of the crates.

They worked quickly, passing the precious cargo down to waiting Resistance fighters. Jack was just handing off the last crate when a bullet pinged off the truck's frame, inches from his head.

"Sniper!" Marianne cried, dragging Jack down into cover.

Jack cursed, peering cautiously around the edge of the truck. He caught a glint of light off a scope in the trees above the ravine. "There," he said, pointing. "Can you see him?"

Marianne squinted, then nodded. "I see him. Cover me."

Before Jack could protest, she was moving, darting from cover to cover with a grace that belied the danger. He provided suppressing fire, his heart in his throat as he watched her close in on the sniper's position.

There was a moment of tense silence, then a single shot rang out. Jack held his breath, every muscle tense. Then Marianne's voice came over the radio, tight with controlled excitement. "Target neutralized. We're clear."

Jack allowed himself a moment of relief before refocusing on the task at hand. "All units, begin exfil," he ordered into his radio. "Rendezvous at point Bravo. Move it, people!"

The withdrawal was a blur of controlled chaos. Jack found himself bringing up the rear, ensuring every member of the assault team made it out. As he reached the edge of the forest, he paused, looking back at the scene of devastation they'd left behind.

The convoy was a smoking ruin, German soldiers milling about in confusion. In the distance, he could hear the wail of approaching sirens. They'd struck a significant blow today, he knew. But at what cost?

A hand on his arm startled him from his thoughts. He turned to find Marianne beside him, her face smudged with soot and something that might have been blood.

"We need to go," she said urgently. "Now."

Jack nodded, allowing her to pull him into the sheltering darkness of the trees. They ran, the sounds of pursuit fading behind them as they plunged deeper into the forest.

It was nearly an hour later when they finally reached the rendezvous point – a long-abandoned barn that had become one of the Resistance's many safe houses. As they approached, Jack did a quick headcount, relief washing over him as he realized everyone had made it out.

Henri met them at the door, his weathered face split in a fierce grin. "A great victory, my friends," he said, clapping Jack on the shoulder. "The Boche will not soon forget this day."

Inside, the atmosphere was one of controlled jubilation. Resistance fighters moved about, securing their hard-won prizes and tending to minor injuries. In one corner, Mike and Tom were already poring over the captured radar components, their faces alight with the thrill of discovery.

Jack made his rounds, checking on each member of the team, offering words of praise and encouragement. But even as he went through the familiar motions of post-mission assessment, a part of his mind was elsewhere, gnawing at a problem that refused to be ignored.

It wasn't until much later, as the adrenaline of the raid began to fade, that he was able to put his finger on what was bothering him. He found Marianne outside, leaning against the weathered barn wall and staring up at the stars just beginning to fade in the lightening sky.

"Penny for your thoughts," he said softly, coming to stand beside her.

She turned to him, a small smile playing at the corners of her mouth. "I was just thinking... about home. About the vineyard." A shadow passed over her face. "I wonder if there will be anything left, when this is all over."

Jack felt a pang of sympathy. For all her strength, all her fierce dedication to the cause, Marianne was still a young woman who had lost nearly everything to this war. He reached out, taking her hand in his. "We'll rebuild," he said. "All of it. I promise."

Marianne's fingers tightened around his, and for a moment, they stood in companionable silence. Then Jack spoke again, giving voice to the concern that had been nagging at him. "Marianne," he said carefully. "That sniper... how did you know exactly where he was? The angle was all wrong from where we were. You couldn't have seen him from the truck."

He felt her tense beside him. When she spoke, her voice was carefully neutral. "I got lucky. A guess, really."

Jack turned to face her fully. "No," he said gently. "It wasn't luck. You knew. Somehow, you knew exactly where he'd be." He paused, weighing his next words carefully. "Just like we knew exactly where to hit that convoy. Just like we've known about every German movement for the past week."

Marianne wouldn't meet his eyes. "Jack, I—"

"It's you, isn't it?" he pressed. "You're Marcel's mysterious informant. The one feeding us all this inside information."

For a long moment, Marianne said nothing. Then, with a sigh that seemed to come from the depths of her soul, she nodded. "Yes," she said softly. "It's me."

Jack felt a complex swirl of emotions – relief at finally knowing the truth, admiration for her courage, and a gnawing worry about what this meant. "How?" he asked simply.

Marianne's gaze remained fixed on the distant horizon. "Do you remember Sturmbannführer Richter? The SS officer we captured at the château?"

Jack nodded, a cold feeling settling in his gut as he began to see where this was going.

"He wasn't just any SS officer," Marianne continued. "He was... he was my fiancé. Before the war."

The revelation hit Jack like a physical blow. He opened his mouth to speak, but Marianne pressed on, the words tumbling out as if a dam had broken.

"We met in Paris, at university. He was charming, brilliant... everything a young, naive girl could want. When the war came, he went back to Germany. I thought I'd never see him again. But then..."

"He came back with the occupation forces," Jack finished for her.

Marianne nodded. "He sought me out. Told me he could protect my family, our land. All I had to do was... cooperate." Her voice hardened. "What he didn't know was that by then, I was already working with the Resistance. I saw an opportunity, and I took it."

Jack's mind reeled with the implications. "So all this time, you've been... what? Playing him? Feeding him false information while gleaning real intelligence?"

"Yes," Marianne said simply. "It hasn't been... easy. But it's been effective."

Jack ran a hand through his hair, trying to process it all. "Jesus, Marianne. Do you have any idea how dangerous that is? If he ever found out—"

"He won't," she cut him off, a hint of steel in her voice. "I've been careful. And now that we have him in custody, well..." She trailed off, but the implication was clear.

A thousand questions raced through Jack's mind, but one rose to the forefront. "Why didn't you tell me?" he asked softly. "Why keep this secret, even after everything we've been through?"

Marianne finally turned to look at him, her eyes shining with unshed tears. "Because I was afraid," she whispered. "Afraid of what you'd think of me. Afraid that if you knew the whole truth, you'd..."

She trailed off, but Jack understood. He reached out, gently cupping her face in his hands. "Marianne," he said softly. "Nothing you could tell me would change how I feel about you. Nothing."

For a moment, they stood like that, the weight of secrets finally lifted, the first rays of dawn painting the sky behind them. Then, slowly, inexorably, they came together in a kiss that tasted of relief, of shared danger, of a future suddenly much less certain but infinitely more precious.

As they broke apart, Jack rested his forehead against hers. "No more secrets," he murmured. "Okay? Whatever comes next, we face it together."

Marianne nodded, a small smile playing at her lips. "Together," she agreed.

The sound of approaching footsteps broke the moment. They turned to see Henri approaching, his face grave. "Capitaine," he said. "We've just received word. The Germans... they're mobilizing. It seems our little raid has stirred up the hornet's nest."

Jack straightened, feeling Marianne tense beside him. "How bad?" he asked.

Henri's expression was grim. "Bad," he said simply. "They're bringing in reinforcements from all over the region. Panzer divisions, SS units... they're out for blood."

Jack nodded, his mind already racing with possibilities, with plans and contingencies. He looked at Marianne, saw the same mix of determination and fear he felt reflected in her eyes.

"Well," he said, managing a grim smile. "I guess our clandestine harvest just got a lot more complicated."

As they turned to head back into the barn, to brief the others and prepare for the storm that was coming, Jack couldn't shake the feeling that everything had changed. The stakes had been raised, the danger multiplied. But as he felt Marianne's hand slip into his, he also knew one thing with absolute certainty.

Whatever came next, they would face it together. And somehow, that made all the difference in the world.

ᛈᛈᛈ

12

London's Secret Room

The incessant drone of air raid sirens pierced the foggy London night, a haunting wail that had become all too familiar to the city's war-weary inhabitants. In a nondescript building just off Whitehall, deep below street level, Jack Holloway stood before a group of stern-faced men, the weight of recent events heavy on his shoulders.

"Gentlemen," he began, his voice steady despite the exhaustion that threatened to overwhelm him, "the situation in occupied France has reached a critical juncture. Our recent operations have dealt significant blows to German infrastructure, but the cost has been high. The enemy is mobilizing on a scale we haven't seen since the initial invasion."

Around the circular table, faces remained impassive, but Jack could sense the tension in the air. These were men accustomed to making life-and-death decisions, to weighing the fate of nations in the balance. But even they seemed sobered by the gravity of the report.

An older man with a neatly trimmed mustache - Air Marshal Sir Douglas Everton, if Jack remembered correctly - leaned forward. "And you're certain of this intelligence,

Captain? The source is reliable?"

Jack hesitated for a fraction of a second, Marianne's face flashing through his mind. "Yes, sir," he said firmly. "The source has proven consistently accurate. We have multiple confirmations of Panzer divisions moving into the region, along with elite SS units. They're not just looking to restore order - they're preparing for a major offensive."

A murmur ran through the room. Another man - civilian clothes, but with the unmistakable bearing of intelligence services - spoke up. "This complicates matters considerably. If the Germans commit significant forces to rooting out the Resistance, it could disrupt our entire timetable for the invasion."

Jack nodded grimly. "That's my assessment as well, sir. The Maquis have been instrumental in gathering intelligence and disrupting German operations. If they're wiped out or forced to go completely underground, we lose a critical asset."

Sir Douglas stroked his mustache thoughtfully. "What do you propose, Captain? Surely you didn't come all this way just to deliver bad news."

"No, sir," Jack replied, straightening. "I have a plan. But I won't pretend it's not risky."

He moved to a large map of France pinned to the wall, indicating a region just south of Paris. "The Germans are consolidating their forces here, at an old château that's been converted into a regional headquarters. Our intelligence suggests that the operational plans for the coming offensive are being coordinated from this location."

Jack turned back to face the room. "I propose a raid. A small team, inserted covertly, to infiltrate the château and either capture or destroy those plans. Without them, the German offensive will be delayed, possibly even called off entirely."

The room erupted in a cacophony of voices, some supportive, others vehemently opposed. Jack stood his ground, waiting for the storm to pass.

Finally, a voice cut through the din. "Enough."

All eyes turned to the far end of the table, where a figure sat half-hidden in shadow. As he leaned forward into the light, Jack recognized him with a jolt of surprise. Winston Churchill, the Prime Minister himself, fixed Jack with a penetrating stare.

"It's a bold plan, Captain," Churchill said, his distinctive voice filling the room. "Some might say foolhardy. But boldness, properly directed, is exactly what this war needs." He paused, puffing thoughtfully on his ever-present cigar. "Tell me, what are your chances of success?"

Jack met the Prime Minister's gaze squarely. "Honestly, sir? I'd say about 30 percent. Maybe less. But if we do nothing, the chances of preserving our intelligence network in France drop to zero."

Churchill nodded slowly. "The stakes are high indeed. Very well, Captain. You have my authorization to proceed. But I want it understood - this operation is completely deniable. If you're captured, His Majesty's Government will disavow all knowledge of your actions. Is that clear?"

"Crystal clear, sir," Jack replied, a mix of relief and trepidation washing over him.

As the meeting adjourned and the various officials filed out, Jack found himself alone with Sir Douglas. The Air Marshal regarded him with a mixture of admiration and concern.

"That was quite a performance, Holloway," he said. "I hope you know what you're getting yourself into."

Jack managed a wry smile. "With all due respect, sir, I don't think any of us truly know what we're getting into in this war. We just do our best and hope it's enough."

Sir Douglas chuckled humorlessly. "Well said. Now, come with me. There's someone you need to meet."

Curious, Jack followed the Air Marshal through a series of winding corridors, descending even deeper beneath the streets of London. They came to a heavy steel door, guarded by two stone-faced MPs. Sir Douglas nodded to them, and the door swung open with a pneumatic hiss.

Beyond lay a room unlike anything Jack had ever seen. Banks of complex machinery lined the walls, their purpose a mystery to him. In the center stood a massive table, upon which was projected a detailed, three-dimensional map of France. Figures moved across its surface, updating in real-time as reports came in from the field.

But it was the woman standing at the table that drew Jack's attention. She was perhaps in her late thirties, with sharp features and penetrating green eyes that seemed to look right through him. Her uniform bore the insignia of British Intelligence, but there was something about her bearing that suggested a authority beyond her apparent rank.

"Captain Holloway," Sir Douglas said, "allow me to introduce Commander Evelyn Maverick. She'll be overseeing the intelligence aspects of your operation."

Jack extended his hand, which Commander Maverick shook with a grip that was surprisingly strong. "A pleasure, Commander," he said.

"Likewise, Captain," she replied, her accent crisp and unmistakably upper-crust. "I've read your reports with great interest. Your work in France has been... most impressive."

There was something in her tone that put Jack on edge. It wasn't quite suspicion, but there was a probing quality to her gaze that made him feel as if he were being dissected.

"Thank you, ma'am," he said cautiously. "I have an excellent team."

"Yes, about that team," Commander Maverick said, moving to the map table. With a few deft movements, she zoomed in on the region where Jack had been operating. "Your reports mention a number of local Resistance fighters. One in particular seems to feature prominently. Marianne Dupont, I believe?"

Jack felt a chill run down his spine. He kept his face carefully neutral as he replied, "That's correct. Mademoiselle Dupont has been an invaluable asset to our operations."

Commander Maverick's eyes never left his face. "I'm sure she has. Tell me, Captain, how much do you really know about her background? Her... connections?"

Jack's mind raced. How much did Maverick know? How much should he reveal? He decided to err on the side of caution. "I know she's been working with the Resistance since the early days of the occupation. Her family has deep roots in the region, which has given us access to a wide network of informants."

Maverick nodded slowly. "All true, I'm sure. But there's more, isn't there? Something you've left out of your official reports."

For a moment, Jack considered continuing to play dumb. But something in Maverick's expression told him that would be a mistake. He took a deep breath. "Alright. What do you want to know?"

A ghost of a smile played at the corners of Maverick's mouth. "That's better. Let's start with Sturmbannführer

Klaus Richter, shall we? I believe you're holding him prisoner?"

Jack nodded, his unease growing. "That's correct. He was captured during our raid on Château Espérance."

"And his relationship with Mademoiselle Dupont? You're aware of it?"

"I am," Jack said carefully. "She informed me of their... history... after his capture."

Maverick's eyes narrowed slightly. "I see. And it didn't occur to you that this might be information your superiors would find relevant?"

Jack felt a flash of anger. "With all due respect, Commander, I made a judgment call. Marianne has proven her loyalty to the Allied cause time and time again. Her past relationship with Richter is just that - past."

"Is it?" Maverick asked softly. She tapped a few commands into the map table, and a series of documents appeared, hovering in the air above the terrain. "We've been monitoring Richter for some time, Captain. His communications, his movements. And do you know what we found?"

Jack said nothing, a sense of dread growing in the pit of his stomach.

"Regular encrypted transmissions," Maverick continued. "To and from the very region where you've been operating. Transmissions that align suspiciously well with your recent successes against German forces."

The implication hit Jack like a physical blow. "You think Marianne is a double agent," he said, his voice barely above a whisper.

Maverick's expression softened slightly. "I think, Captain, that the situation is far more complex than your reports have indicated. I think you've allowed your...

personal feelings... to cloud your judgment."

Jack opened his mouth to protest, but Maverick held up a hand to stop him. "I'm not here to judge you, Captain. God knows, in this war, the lines between ally and enemy, love and duty, have become blurred beyond recognition. But the fact remains - we cannot proceed with this operation until we know exactly where Mademoiselle Dupont's loyalties lie."

For a long moment, Jack said nothing, his mind whirling with the implications of what he'd just heard. Finally, he looked up, meeting Maverick's gaze. "What do you want me to do?"

Maverick's expression was grave. "When you return to France, you will continue with the mission as planned. But you will also have a secondary objective. You are to extract Mademoiselle Dupont and bring her back to London for... debriefing."

Jack felt as if the floor had dropped out from under him. "You want me to kidnap her," he said flatly.

"I want you to secure a valuable intelligence asset," Maverick corrected. "One way or another, we need to know the full extent of her involvement with Richter and the German high command."

"And if she resists?" Jack asked, dreading the answer.

Maverick's eyes were cold. "Then you are authorized to use whatever means necessary to ensure her cooperation. Am I clear, Captain?"

Jack stood frozen, the weight of the impossible choice before him pressing down like a physical force. Everything in him rebelled against the idea of betraying Marianne's trust. But if there was even a chance that she was working for the Germans...

"Captain Holloway," Maverick's voice cut through his turmoil. "I asked you a question. Am I clear?"

Jack took a deep breath, squaring his shoulders. When he spoke, his voice was steady, betraying none of the conflict raging within him. "Yes, Commander. Crystal clear."

Maverick nodded, seemingly satisfied. "Good. You'll be briefed on the full details of the extraction plan before you leave. For now, get some rest. You leave for France at 0600 hours."

As Jack turned to go, Maverick's voice stopped him once more. "And Captain? Remember - the fate of the entire invasion could rest on the success of this mission. Personal feelings cannot be allowed to interfere. Is that understood?"

Jack didn't turn around. He couldn't bear to meet her gaze, afraid of what she might see in his eyes. "Understood, Commander," he said quietly. Then he was gone, the door of the secret room closing behind him with a finality that felt like the slamming of a prison cell.

As he made his way back through the labyrinthine corridors of the underground complex, Jack's mind raced. How had it come to this? Just days ago, he had been in France, fighting alongside people he trusted, working towards a common goal. Now... now everything was cast in shadow, every relationship tinged with suspicion.

He thought of Marianne - her fierce determination, her unwavering courage in the face of danger. Could it all have been an act? A long con played out over months, years even? The rational part of his mind knew it was possible. The intelligence game was built on such deceptions, after all. But his heart... his heart rebelled against the very idea.

As he emerged onto the darkened streets of London, the air raid sirens still wailing their mournful warning, Jack felt more alone than he had since the war began. The weight of secrets, of impossible choices, pressed down on him like a physical force.

Tomorrow, he would return to France. To his team, to the Resistance fighters who had become like family. To Marianne. And he would carry with him a burden that threatened to tear apart everything they had built.

Jack looked up at the searchlights crisscrossing the sky, seeking out the German bombers that even now were on their way to rain destruction down on the city. In that moment, he made a silent vow. Whatever the truth turned out to be, whatever choices lay ahead, he would not let this war destroy what was good and true in the world. He would find a way to navigate the treacherous waters ahead, to protect those he cared about while still serving the greater cause.

As he walked through the eerily quiet streets, Jack steeled himself for the challenges to come. London's secret room had changed everything. But some secrets, he knew, were worth keeping - even at the cost of one's soul.

꧁꧁꧁

13
Return to the Skies

The belly of the RAF Halifax bomber groaned and shuddered as it fought its way through the turbulent night sky over occupied France. Jack Holloway sat in the cramped fuselage, surrounded by the quiet tension of his team. Mike and Tom flanked him, their faces masks of concentration as they mentally rehearsed the mission ahead. Across from them, two new additions to the team – a wiry demolitions expert named Cooper and a taciturn radio operator called Singh – checked their equipment with meticulous care.

Jack's mind, however, was far from the immediate dangers of their nighttime insertion. Commander Maverick's words echoed in his head, a persistent whisper that drowned out even the roar of the bomber's engines.

"Extract Mademoiselle Dupont... bring her back to London for debriefing... whatever means necessary..."

He closed his eyes, trying to center himself. The mission was already dangerous enough without the added complication of potentially having to betray one of their own. But was Marianne truly one of them? The seed of doubt planted in London's secret room had taken root, growing into a twisted tangle of suspicion and uncertainty.

A hand on his shoulder startled Jack from his brooding. He looked up to see Mike watching him with concern.

"You alright, boss?" the lieutenant shouted over the engine noise. "You look like you're about a million miles away."

Jack managed a tight smile. "Just going over the plan," he lied. "Lot of moving parts on this one."

Mike nodded, though his expression suggested he wasn't entirely convinced. "We've got this, Jack. The team's solid, the intel is good. We'll be in and out before the Krauts know what hit them."

Jack wished he could share his friend's confidence. But the "good intel" Mike spoke of was precisely what worried him. How much of it had come from Marianne? And how much of that could they truly trust?

Before he could dwell further on these dark thoughts, the red light above the jump door flashed on. The loadmaster, a grizzled RAF sergeant, gave them a thumbs up.

"Two minutes to drop zone!" he bellowed.

The team rose as one, checking parachutes and weapons one last time. Jack felt the familiar surge of adrenaline, the mix of fear and exhilaration that came with every jump. For a moment, all thoughts of London, of Maverick, of Marianne's potential betrayal faded away. There was only the mission.

The light turned green. The jump door swung open, letting in a blast of frigid air.

"Go! Go! Go!" Jack shouted.

One by one, they leapt into the darkness. Jack was last, pausing for a heartbeat at the threshold. Then he was falling, the wind tearing at his face as the earth rushed up to meet him.

The free fall seemed to last both an eternity and no time at all. Jack's mind cleared, focused solely on the immediate task of survival. At the right moment, he pulled his ripcord. The jolt as his parachute deployed nearly knocked the wind out of him, but he managed to control his descent, guiding himself towards the planned landing zone.

As the ground approached, Jack could make out the shadowy forms of his team already on the ground, quickly gathering their chutes. He braced for impact, hitting the earth with a bone-jarring thud and immediately rolling to disperse the energy of the landing.

For a tense few moments, the only sound was the rustle of parachutes being hastily bundled and buried. Then Mike's voice came over the radio, barely above a whisper.

"All present and accounted for, Captain. No signs of German patrols in the immediate vicinity."

Jack allowed himself a small sigh of relief. Phase one complete. Now came the hard part.

They moved swiftly through the darkened countryside, using the cover of a moonless night to their advantage. The rendezvous point was a small farmhouse about three kilometers from their landing zone – a safe house operated by the local Resistance.

As they approached, Jack felt his tension ratchet up another notch. Would Marianne be there? And if she was, how would he handle the impossible task Maverick had set for him?

A soft whistle cut through the night – the prearranged signal. Jack returned it, then watched as a figure materialized from the shadows near the farmhouse. His heart skipped a beat as he recognized the lithe form of Marianne Dupont.

"Bienvenue, mes amis," she said softly as they drew near. "I trust your trip was uneventful?"

Jack nodded, not trusting himself to speak just yet. He searched her face, looking for... what? Some sign of deception? Some hint that would confirm or dispel his doubts? But all he saw was the same fierce determination, the same warmth in her eyes when they met his.

"Come," Marianne said, gesturing towards the farmhouse. "The others are waiting. We have much to discuss."

Inside, they found Eduard Dupont and Henri, the grizzled Maquis leader, poring over maps spread across a rickety kitchen table. Both men looked up as the team entered, their faces a mixture of relief and grim determination.

"Capitaine," Henri greeted Jack with a firm handshake. "It is good to see you again. Though I wish it were under better circumstances."

Jack nodded, understanding all too well. The German response to their recent operations had been swift and brutal. Villages suspected of harboring Resistance fighters had been razed, civilians executed as examples. The stakes of their mission had never been higher.

As the team settled in, accepting cups of bitter ersatz coffee and stale bread, Jack gave a brief overview of the plan. The German headquarters at Château Rothschild, the critical intelligence believed to be housed there, the narrow window of opportunity they had to strike.

Throughout the briefing, Jack was acutely aware of Marianne's presence. She listened intently, occasionally offering insights on German patrol patterns or the layout of the château. Each piece of information she provided sent a fresh wave of conflict through Jack. Was this the input of a dedicated ally? Or the carefully crafted manipulations of a double agent?

As the briefing concluded and the team broke into smaller groups to discuss specific aspects of the operation, Jack found himself alone with Marianne for the first time since his return from London. She must have sensed his unease, for her brow furrowed with concern.

"Jack? What is it? You seem... distant."

He struggled to meet her gaze, the weight of his secret mission pressing down on him. "It's nothing," he lied. "Just... the pressure of what we're about to do. A lot riding on this one."

Marianne's hand found his, her touch sending an electric current through him. "We will succeed," she said with quiet conviction. "We have to. For France. For all of us."

The sincerity in her voice made Jack's heart ache. How could he doubt her? How could he even consider the possibility that she might be working against them? And yet... Maverick's warnings echoed in his mind. The encrypted transmissions. The suspiciously accurate intelligence.

"Marianne," he began, not sure what he was going to say but knowing he had to say something. "I need to ask you—"

He was cut off by a commotion outside. Shouts in German, the sound of vehicles approaching fast.

"Merde!" Henri cursed, rushing to the window. "German patrol! They must have spotted your chutes!"

In an instant, the farmhouse erupted into controlled chaos. Weapons were grabbed, maps hastily rolled up and stuffed into packs. Jack's mind raced, assessing options, calculating risks.

"The cellar," Eduard said urgently. "There's a hidden passage, leads to a cave system in the hills. We can lose them there."

As the team hurried to gather their gear, Jack caught Marianne's arm. "Wait," he said, his voice low and intense. "I need to know. The intelligence you've been providing... where does it come from? How can you be so sure it's accurate?"

Surprise and hurt flashed across Marianne's face. "You're asking me this now? Jack, what's gotten into you?"

The sound of boots on gravel outside grew louder. They were out of time.

"Just... tell me," Jack pressed. "Please. I need to know I can trust you."

For a moment, Marianne said nothing. Then her expression hardened into something Jack had never seen before – a mixture of determination and what might have been regret.

"You want the truth?" she said, her voice barely above a whisper. "Fine. But not here. Not now. When we're clear of this, I'll tell you everything. I promise."

Before Jack could respond, Mike's urgent voice cut through the tension. "Captain! We need to move, now!"

With one last, lingering look at Marianne, Jack turned away. "Alright, people, let's go! Down to the cellar, move it!"

They filed down the narrow stairs just as the first pounding on the farmhouse door began. Jack brought up the rear, his mind whirling with conflicting emotions. As Eduard pulled the hidden lever that revealed the secret passage, Jack couldn't shake the feeling that they were descending into more than just a physical darkness.

The passage was cramped and damp, forcing them to move in single file. Jack could hear the muffled sounds of German voices above, the thud of boots as the patrol searched the now-empty farmhouse. His hand tightened on his weapon, every nerve on high alert.

They emerged into a larger cavern, dimly lit by the flashlights carried by Henri and Eduard. The Maquis leader consulted a crude map etched into the cave wall.

"This way," he whispered. "There's an exit about two kilometers from here. Should put us well clear of the German search area."

As they made their way through the twisting passages, Jack found himself next to Marianne once more. The tension between them was palpable, a nearly physical force in the close confines of the cave.

"Jack," she began, her voice low. "About what you asked earlier—"

He cut her off with a sharp gesture. "Not now. We need to focus on getting out of here alive. But after... we will talk."

Marianne nodded, a flicker of something – resignation? resolve? – passing across her face in the dim light.

The journey through the caves seemed to stretch on for hours, though Jack's watch told him it had been less than forty minutes. Finally, they reached a narrow fissure that opened onto a wooded hillside. The first faint light of dawn was just beginning to paint the eastern sky.

"We're clear," Henri announced after a tense few minutes of observation. "No sign of German patrols in the area."

A collective sigh of relief went through the group. They had escaped, for now. But the close call had driven home the precariousness of their situation. The Germans were on high alert, actively hunting for them. The window for their mission was rapidly closing.

As the team regrouped, discussing their next move, Jack pulled Marianne aside. The time for secrets was over.

"Alright," he said, keeping his voice low but unable to entirely mask the intensity of his feelings. "We're clear. Now tell me the truth. All of it."

Marianne met his gaze steadily, a mix of emotions playing across her face – defiance, fear, and something else Jack couldn't quite identify.

"Very well," she said softly. "But you may not like what you hear."

She took a deep breath, as if steeling herself for what was to come. "The intelligence I've been providing... it comes from Klaus. From Sturmbannführer Richter."

Jack felt as if he'd been punched in the gut. "You've been in contact with him? All this time?"

Marianne nodded, her expression pained. "It's not what you think. Klaus... he's not like the others. He never truly believed in the Nazi ideology. When he was assigned to our region, he sought me out. Not just because of our past, but because he wanted to help."

Jack's mind reeled. "Help? He's an SS officer, Marianne. How could you possibly trust him?"

"Because I know him," Marianne said fiercely. "I know his heart. He's been feeding us information, using his position to misdirect German efforts against the Resistance. When we captured him at the château... it was part of the plan. To cement his cover, to make the Germans believe he was truly our enemy."

The pieces began to fall into place in Jack's mind – the suspiciously accurate intelligence, the encrypted transmissions Maverick had mentioned. But one crucial question remained.

"Why didn't you tell me?" he asked, unable to keep the hurt from his voice. "Why keep this secret, even from me?"

Marianne's eyes glistened with unshed tears. "Because I knew how it would look. Because I was afraid... afraid you wouldn't understand. Afraid you'd see me as a traitor."

Jack ran a hand through his hair, his emotions a turbulent mix of relief, confusion, and lingering doubt. "I don't know what to think, Marianne. This is... it's a lot to take in."

She reached out, taking his hand in hers. "I know. And I'm sorry for not telling you sooner. But Jack, you have to believe me. Everything I've done, everything Klaus has done, has been in service of the Resistance. Of freeing France."

Jack looked into her eyes, searching for any sign of deception. But all he saw was sincerity, and a depth of feeling that took his breath away.

Before he could respond, Mike's voice cut through the moment. "Captain! We've got movement on the ridge. Looks like the Germans have picked up our trail."

Reality came crashing back. Whatever the truth of Marianne's revelation, whatever it meant for them, for the mission, it would have to wait. Right now, they had a job to do.

Jack squeezed Marianne's hand once, then turned to face his team. "Alright, people, change of plans. We move now, hit the château hard and fast. No more time for subtlety."

As the team gathered their gear, preparing for what might be their most dangerous operation yet, Jack cast one last glance at Marianne. She met his gaze steadily, a world of unspoken words passing between them.

Whatever came next, Jack knew one thing for certain – their return to the skies had been just the beginning. The real test, for all of them, lay ahead.

ᗥᗥᗥ

14

Shadows in the Village

Dawn's first light struggled to penetrate the thick fog enveloping Saint-Clair-sur-Epte, casting eerie shadows across cobblestone streets that had witnessed centuries of history. Jack Holloway crouched in the shadow of a crumbling stone wall, his team spread out around him in strategic positions. The village, once a picturesque snapshot of rural French life, now felt like a powder keg ready to explode.

Marianne's revelation about Sturmbannführer Richter still echoed in Jack's mind, a dissonant chord that refused to resolve. But there was no time to dwell on it now. They had a mission to complete, and the sudden appearance of German patrols had forced them to adapt their plans on the fly.

"Mike, what's your status?" Jack whispered into his radio.

"All quiet on the western front, boss," came the lieutenant's hushed reply. "But I've got a bad feeling about this. It's too quiet."

Jack nodded grimly, even though Mike couldn't see him. The oppressive silence of the village was unnatural, eerie. Where were the early risers, the farmers heading out to their fields? The usual sounds of a village coming to life were conspicuously absent.

A soft rustle to his left announced Marianne's approach. She slid into cover beside him, her face a mask of tension and barely contained energy.

"Jack," she said, her voice barely above a whisper, "something's wrong. I've been watching the baker's shop. It should have opened an hour ago, but there's no sign of life."

Jack felt a chill that had nothing to do with the pre-dawn chill. "You think the Germans have cleared the village?"

Marianne's expression darkened. "It's possible. But why? And where would they take everyone?"

Before Jack could respond, Tom's urgent voice crackled over the radio. "Captain, we've got movement. Nordwest corner of the village. Looks like a German patrol, but... something's off."

"Define 'off,' Lieutenant," Jack replied, already moving to get a better vantage point.

"They're... herding people. Civilians. Looks like they're gathering them in the town square."

Jack exchanged a loaded glance with Marianne. This changed everything. Their plan to use the village as a staging ground for their assault on Château Rothschild was now completely untenable. But more than that, they couldn't simply stand by and watch innocent civilians being rounded up.

"All units, hold position," Jack ordered. "We need more intel before we make a move. Tom, can you get eyes on the square without being spotted?"

"Affirmative, Captain. Moving now."

The next few minutes stretched into an eternity as they waited for Tom's report. Jack could feel the tension radiating off Marianne in waves. He knew she must be thinking of her friends and neighbors, people she'd known her entire life, now at the mercy of the Nazi occupiers.

Finally, Tom's voice returned, tight with barely contained anger. "It's bad, sir. They've got the whole village out there. Men, women, children. And... Christ, they're separating them into groups. Looks like they're selecting the able-bodied men and some of the younger women."

"Forced labor," Marianne hissed, her hands clenching into fists. "Or worse."

Jack's mind raced, weighing options, calculating risks. Their primary mission was critical – the intelligence at Château Rothschild could potentially save thousands of lives and significantly impact the course of the war. But could they in good conscience abandon these villagers to their fate?

"Sir," Mike's voice cut through Jack's deliberations. "I hate to add to our problems, but we've got another issue. I just spotted Richter."

Jack felt Marianne stiffen beside him. "Sturmbannführer Richter? Here?"

"Affirmative," Mike confirmed. "He just arrived in a staff car. Looks like he's overseeing the whole operation."

Jack turned to Marianne, searching her face for... what? Some sign of divided loyalties? Some hint of the truth behind her claims about Richter's secret allegiance? But all he saw was a mixture of fear and fierce determination.

"We have to do something," she said, her voice low and intense. "Jack, these are my people. We can't just—"

"I know," he cut her off, his tone gentler than he'd intended. "And we will. But we need to be smart about this. One wrong move and we could get a lot of innocent people killed."

Jack keyed his radio again. "All units, converge on my position. We need to regroup and come up with a new plan."

As the team gathered in the shelter of an abandoned barn on the outskirts of the village, Jack could feel the weight of expectation on his shoulders. These men – and Marianne – were looking to him for answers, for a way out of this impossible situation.

"Alright," he began, his voice low but firm. "Here's what we know. The Germans have rounded up the entire village population. They're separating them, likely for forced labor or deportation. Sturmbannführer Richter is overseeing the operation personally."

He paused, letting the gravity of the situation sink in. "Our primary mission remains critical. The intel at Château Rothschild could potentially turn the tide of the entire war effort in this region. But," he held up a hand to forestall the objections he could see forming on several faces, "we also have a responsibility to these civilians. We can't simply abandon them to whatever fate the Nazis have in store."

"So what's the play, boss?" Mike asked, his usual easygoing manner replaced by grim determination.

Jack took a deep breath. "We split up. Mike, you'll take Cooper and Singh. Your job is to continue with the original mission. Infiltrate Château Rothschild, secure the intelligence, and get out. Radio silence unless absolutely necessary."

Mike nodded, though Jack could see the reluctance in his eyes. "And the rest of us?"

"We stay here," Jack said. "Tom, Henri, Marianne, and I will work on a plan to disrupt the German operation and free as many villagers as we can."

"It's too risky," Eduard interjected, speaking up for the first time. "If we split our forces, both missions could fail.

And if we're captured..." He left the rest unsaid, but they all knew the implications. Torture, execution, and the compromise of the entire Resistance network in the region.

Jack met the older man's gaze steadily. "It's a risk we have to take. We can't abandon these people, and we can't lose the intelligence at the château. Sometimes, the only way forward is to make the impossible choice."

A heavy silence fell over the group. Jack could see the conflict playing out on each face – the desire to help, warring with the cold logic of wartime priorities.

Finally, Marianne spoke up. "Jack's right," she said, her voice quiet but filled with resolve. "We have to try. These are our people, our neighbors. If we turn our backs on them now, what are we even fighting for?"

Her words seemed to galvanize the group. Nods of agreement rippled through the team, and Jack felt a surge of pride and affection for this fierce, compassionate woman.

"Alright," he said, allowing a hint of a smile to touch his lips. "Let's get to work. Mike, get your team ready. You move out in ten minutes. The rest of us, we need to come up with a plan to create maximum chaos with minimal civilian casualties."

As the group broke up to prepare, Jack pulled Marianne aside. "There's something else we need to discuss," he said quietly. "Richter."

Marianne's expression tightened, but she nodded. "What about him?"

"If what you told me is true, if he really is working against the Nazis from the inside, then he might be our best chance at resolving this without bloodshed."

"You want to make contact," Marianne said. It wasn't a question.

Jack nodded. "Can you do it? Safely?"

For a long moment, Marianne said nothing, her gaze distant as she weighed the risks. Finally, she met Jack's eyes. "Yes," she said simply. "But Jack, you have to understand. If we do this, if we reveal Richter's true allegiance, we burn one of our most valuable assets. The intelligence he's been providing—"

"Won't mean a damn thing if we let these people be carted off to labor camps or worse," Jack finished for her. "I know it's a high price, Marianne. But right now, it might be our only play."

Marianne closed her eyes briefly, as if steeling herself for what was to come. When she opened them again, they were filled with a fierce determination that took Jack's breath away.

"Alright," she said. "I'll do it. But Jack, promise me something."

"Anything," he replied without hesitation.

"If this goes wrong, if Richter betrays us or if the Germans overwhelm us... promise me you'll complete the mission. Get to the château, get the intelligence. No matter what happens to me or the villagers."

Jack felt as if he'd been punched in the gut. The thought of leaving Marianne behind, of abandoning these innocent people to their fate, was almost unbearable. But he knew she was right. The stakes were too high, the potential impact of their mission too great.

"I promise," he said softly, hating himself for the words even as he spoke them.

Marianne nodded, a sad smile touching her lips. Then, in a move that caught Jack completely off guard, she leaned in and kissed him. It was brief, desperate, filled with all the things they'd left unsaid.

When she pulled away, her eyes were shining with unshed tears. "For luck," she said, her voice barely above a whisper.

Before Jack could respond, she was gone, slipping away into the shadows of the village. He watched her go, his heart a turbulent mix of emotions. Then, with a deep breath, he turned back to the task at hand.

The next hour was a blur of furtive movement and tense preparations. Jack coordinated with Tom and Henri, setting up improvised explosive devices at key points around the village. If things went south, they'd need every advantage they could get.

All the while, his mind was on Marianne. Had she made contact with Richter? Was she safe? And perhaps most troublingly, could they truly trust the SS officer, regardless of Marianne's assurances?

As the first rays of dawn began to paint the eastern sky, Jack found himself crouched once more at the edge of the village square. The scene before him was one of controlled chaos. German soldiers stood in a perimeter, their weapons trained on the huddled groups of villagers. At the center of it all stood Sturmbannführer Richter, his crisp black uniform a stark contrast to the disheveled civilians.

Jack's radio crackled to life. "Captain," Mike's voice came through, tense but controlled. "We're in position at the château. Awaiting your go/no-go."

Jack took a deep breath. This was it. The point of no return. Whatever happened in the next few minutes would determine the fate of not just this village, but potentially the entire war effort in the region.

"Stand by, Lieutenant," he replied. "We're about to—"

His words were cut off by a sudden commotion in the square. Jack's heart leapt into his throat as he saw Marianne striding purposefully towards Richter, her hands raised in a gesture of surrender.

"Halt!" Richter's voice rang out, sharp and commanding. "Mademoiselle Dupont. To what do we owe this... unexpected pleasure?"

Marianne's voice, when she spoke, was clear and unwavering. "I've come to negotiate, Herr Sturmbannführer. For the lives of these people. And... to deliver a message."

Jack watched, barely daring to breathe, as Marianne leaned in close to Richter, whispering something in his ear. The SS officer's expression remained impassive, but Jack thought he saw a flicker of... something... in the man's eyes.

For a long, tense moment, nothing happened. Jack's finger tightened on the trigger of his weapon, ready to unleash hell if Richter made a move against Marianne.

Then, slowly, deliberately, Richter turned to his subordinates. "Release them," he ordered, his voice carrying clearly across the square. "All of them. We've received new intelligence. These people are to be left in peace."

A ripple of confusion went through the German soldiers, but they obeyed, lowering their weapons and beginning to herd the stunned villagers back towards their homes.

Jack could scarcely believe what he was seeing. Had Marianne's gambit actually worked? Had Richter truly been on their side all along?

But even as relief began to wash over him, Jack saw something that made his blood run cold. A German officer, standing just behind Richter, was reaching for his sidearm, his face a mask of suspicion and rage.

Time seemed to slow. Jack saw the glint of metal as the pistol cleared its holster. He saw Marianne's eyes widen as she realized the danger. And he saw Richter, turning too late to stop what was about to happen.

Without conscious thought, Jack was moving. He burst from cover, his own weapon raised. "Marianne!" he shouted. "Down!"

The square erupted into chaos. Jack's first shot took the German officer in the shoulder, spinning him around. But not before the man's pistol barked once, twice.

Marianne crumpled to the ground. Richter staggered, red blossoming on his immaculate uniform.

And all around them, the shadows of the village exploded into violent, terrifying light.

ϸϸϸ

15
Cracks in the Ranks

Oberst Wilhelm Müller stood at the window of his office in Château Rothschild, his steely gaze fixed on the distant horizon where the first rays of dawn were just beginning to paint the sky. Behind him, the opulent room — once a showcase of French aristocratic excess, now converted into a sterile military command center — buzzed with the quiet efficiency of his staff.

But Müller's mind was far from the routine reports and logistics of running the German occupation in this region of France. His thoughts were consumed by a growing suspicion, a nagging doubt that refused to be silenced.

"Hauptmann," he called, not turning from the window. "Bring me the latest intelligence reports on Resistance activities in the area. And the personnel file on Sturmbannführer Richter."

"Jawohl, Herr Oberst," came the crisp reply. A moment later, a young officer approached, arms laden with folders.

Müller turned, fixing the captain with a penetrating stare. "Tell me, Hauptmann Bauer, what do you make of our recent... setbacks against the local Resistance?"

Bauer shifted uncomfortably under his superior's gaze. "Sir, the terrorists have been unusually well-informed and coordinated in their attacks. Our losses have been... significant."

"Indeed," Müller mused, taking the folders and beginning to leaf through them. "And what of Sturmbannführer Richter's role in all this? His performance has been... curious, wouldn't you say?"

"Sir?" Bauer's voice held a note of confusion, and perhaps a hint of fear. Questioning the loyalty of an SS officer was dangerous territory.

Müller's lips thinned into a grim smile. "Come now, Hauptmann. Surely you've noticed. The Resistance always seems to be one step ahead of Richter's operations. His captures yield little useful intelligence. And now this business in Saint-Clair-sur-Epte..."

He trailed off, his eyes scanning a report detailing the events of the previous night. The sudden appearance of a known Resistance member — Marianne Dupont — followed by Richter's inexplicable order to release all the detained villagers. And then, chaos. Gunfire. Explosions.

"Sir," Bauer ventured cautiously, "the latest radio intercepts suggest that both Sturmbannführer Richter and the Dupont woman were wounded in the incident. They're believed to be in Resistance custody now."

Müller's eyebrow arched. "Are they indeed? How very... convenient."

He turned back to the window, his mind working furiously. The pieces were beginning to fall into place, forming a picture he found deeply troubling.

"Hauptmann," he said, his voice deceptively calm, "I want a full security review of all operations Richter has been involved in over the past six months. Every mission, every interrogation, every scrap of intelligence. And I want it done quietly. Is that understood?"

"Jawohl, Herr Oberst," Bauer replied, snapping to attention. "And if we find evidence of... irregularities?"

Müller's expression hardened. "Then, Hauptmann, we will clean house. Thoroughly and without mercy."

As Bauer hurried off to carry out his orders, Müller allowed himself a moment of grim satisfaction. If his suspicions were correct, if Richter had indeed turned traitor, then the game was about to change dramatically.

But even as he contemplated the ramifications of such a betrayal, another part of Müller's tactician's mind was already moving on to the next problem. The Resistance had struck a significant blow, yes. But in doing so, they had also exposed themselves. And now, with their precious SS mole potentially compromised, they would be vulnerable.

A predatory smile played at the corners of Müller's mouth. Perhaps it was time to spring a trap of his own.

ᛈᛈᛈ

Miles away, in a hidden Resistance safehouse deep in the French countryside, Jack Holloway paced restlessly. The events of the past 24 hours played on an endless loop in his mind — the chaos in the village square, the shocking revelation of Richter's true allegiance, and most of all, the sickening moment when he saw Marianne fall.

"Jack," Tom's voice cut through his brooding. "You need to rest. You're no good to anyone if you run yourself into the ground."

Jack ran a hand through his hair, frustration evident in every line of his body. "I can't just sit here doing nothing, Tom. Marianne's still in surgery, Richter's status is unknown, and for all we know, the Germans could be closing in on us right now."

Tom laid a comforting hand on his captain's shoulder. "I know. But we've done everything we can for now. The doc's working on Marianne and Richter. Mike's team is still at the château, gathering intel. And Henri's got his people watching every approach to this place. We're as safe as we can be, given the circumstances."

Jack nodded reluctantly, knowing his friend was right but hating the feeling of helplessness that threatened to overwhelm him. He was about to respond when the door to the makeshift infirmary opened.

Dr. Claudette Rousseau emerged, looking exhausted but satisfied. "Captain," she said, her accent thick with fatigue, "I have good news. Mademoiselle Dupont is stable. The bullet missed any vital organs. With rest and care, she should make a full recovery."

Jack felt a wave of relief wash over him. "Thank God," he breathed. "And Richter?"

Dr. Rousseau's expression grew more serious. "His condition is... more complicated. The bullet did considerable damage. I've done what I can, but..." She spread her hands in a helpless gesture. "The next 24 hours will be critical."

Jack nodded, processing this information. Part of him — a dark, angry part he wasn't proud of — almost wished Richter wouldn't pull through. It would certainly simplify things. But he pushed the thought aside. Like it or not, the SS officer was now a valuable asset, one they couldn't afford to lose.

"Can I see her?" he asked, already moving towards the infirmary door.

Dr. Rousseau hesitated, then nodded. "Briefly. But she needs rest, Captain. Try not to excite her."

Jack slipped into the dimly lit room, his eyes immediately finding Marianne's still form on one of the narrow cots. She looked pale and fragile, so unlike the fierce, vibrant woman he knew. But as he approached, her eyes fluttered open, focusing on him with an effort.

"Jack," she murmured, a faint smile touching her lips. "You look terrible."

Despite everything, Jack felt a chuckle escape him. "You're one to talk," he said softly, taking her hand in his. "How are you feeling?"

"Like I've been shot," Marianne replied dryly. Then, more seriously, "Klaus? Is he...?"

Jack's expression tightened. "Alive, for now. It's touch and go."

Marianne closed her eyes briefly, a mix of emotions playing across her face. "He saved my life, Jack. When that officer drew his weapon... Klaus saw it before I did. He pushed me aside, took the bullet meant for me."

Jack felt a complex swirl of emotions at her words — gratitude towards Richter for saving Marianne, mixed with a lingering jealousy he couldn't quite suppress. "I guess we owe him one, then," he said, trying to keep his tone neutral.

Marianne must have sensed something in his voice, for her eyes opened again, fixing him with an intense gaze. "Jack," she said softly, "what happened between Klaus and me... it's in the past. You have to believe that."

"I do," Jack replied, surprising himself with the realization that it was true. "But Marianne, we need to talk about what happens next. Richter's cover is blown. The Germans will be out for blood. And the intel we gathered from the château..." He trailed off, not sure how to continue.

Marianne's grip on his hand tightened. "Tell me," she said, her voice stronger now. "Whatever it is, I can handle it."

Jack took a deep breath. "It's bad. Really bad. The Germans are planning a major offensive, not just against the Resistance, but against civilian targets as well. They're calling it Operation Harvest Moon. Mass deportations, reprisal killings... it's going to be a bloodbath."

Marianne's face paled even further, if that was possible. "Mon Dieu," she whispered. "When?"

"Soon," Jack said grimly. "Within the next 72 hours, according to the documents Mike's team recovered. We're running out of time, Marianne. And now, with you and Richter injured..."

He didn't need to finish the thought. They both knew the implications. Their network was compromised, their resources stretched to the breaking point. And now, facing the largest German operation since the initial invasion, they were woefully unprepared.

Marianne was silent for a long moment, her eyes distant as she processed this information. Then, with visible effort, she pushed herself up into a sitting position, ignoring Jack's protests.

"We need to move," she said, her voice filled with a determination that belied her weakened state. "Get word to every Resistance cell in the region. Evacuate as many civilians as we can. And then..." Her eyes met Jack's, blazing with a fierce light. "Then we fight. With everything we have."

Jack felt a surge of admiration and love for this incredible woman. Even wounded, even in the face of overwhelming odds, she refused to give up.

"Alright," he said, squeezing her hand gently. "But you focus on getting better. I'll coordinate with Henri and the others, start putting a plan together."

Marianne nodded, then pulled Jack closer. "Be careful," she whispered. "And Jack... whatever happens, know that

I—"

She was cut off by a commotion outside. Jack sprang to his feet, his hand going to his weapon as Tom burst into the room.

"Captain," the sergeant said, his face grim. "We've got a problem. Big problem."

"What is it?" Jack demanded, already moving towards the door.

"It's Richter," Tom replied. "He's awake. And he's demanding to speak to you. Says he has critical information about something called Operation Harvest Moon."

Jack exchanged a loaded glance with Marianne. "How the hell does he know about that?"

"I don't know," Tom said, shaking his head. "But that's not all. He says there's a mole, Jack. Someone high up in the Resistance. Someone feeding information directly to a German colonel named Müller."

The room seemed to spin around Jack as the implications of this bombshell sank in. A mole. A traitor in their midst. And if Richter was to be believed, someone with access to their highest levels of command.

"Alright," he said, his mind already racing with possibilities and contingencies. "Tom, get Henri and Eduard. Full security lockdown. No one in or out without my direct authorization. And send Dr. Rousseau to check on Richter. I want to make sure he's stable enough for questioning."

As Tom hurried off to carry out his orders, Jack turned back to Marianne. The look they shared was one of grim understanding. Whatever was coming, whatever revelations and betrayals lay ahead, they would face it together.

"Be careful," Marianne said softly, echoing her earlier words. "If there really is a mole..."

Jack nodded, his expression hardening. "I know. Trust no one." He leaned in, pressing a gentle kiss to her forehead. "Get some rest. I'll be back as soon as I can."

As he strode out of the infirmary, Jack's mind was a whirlwind of conflicting thoughts and emotions. The identity of the mole, the looming threat of Operation Harvest Moon, the precarious state of their entire Resistance network — it all seemed to press down on him with crushing weight.

But beneath it all, there was a core of steely resolve. They had faced impossible odds before and come out on top. They would do so again. They had to. The alternative was unthinkable.

Jack made his way to the room where Richter was being held, nodding to the armed guards posted outside. As he reached for the door handle, he took a deep breath, steeling himself for whatever revelations lay on the other side.

One way or another, he knew, the next few minutes would change everything.

16

The Mole

Jack Holloway stood before the door to Richter's makeshift cell, his hand hovering over the handle. The weight of the moment pressed down on him, a physical force that seemed to make the very air heavy. With a deep breath, he steeled himself and entered.

The room was dim, lit only by a single bare bulb that cast harsh shadows across the walls. Richter lay on a narrow cot, his face pale and drawn with pain. But his eyes, when they met Jack's, were sharp and alert.

"Captain Holloway," Richter said, his voice weak but steady. "I was beginning to think you'd leave me to rot in here."

Jack pulled up a chair, sitting just out of arm's reach of the injured SS officer. "You said you had information about Operation Harvest Moon. And about a mole in the Resistance. Start talking."

Richter's lips curved in a humorless smile. "Always straight to business, eh, Captain? Very well. But first, tell me – how is Marianne?"

Jack felt a flare of irritation, mixed with a grudging respect for the man's concern. "She'll live, no thanks to you and your Nazi friends."

"On the contrary," Richter replied, a hint of steel entering his voice. "If not for me, she'd be dead. I took that bullet for her, Captain. Remember that."

For a moment, the two men stared at each other, a silent battle of wills. Then Jack nodded, conceding the point. "Fair enough. Now, the information. What do you know?"

Richter shifted, wincing as the movement pulled at his wound. "Operation Harvest Moon is worse than you think. It's not just an offensive against the Resistance. It's a scorched earth policy. They plan to destroy everything – crops, infrastructure, entire villages. Anyone suspected of aiding the Resistance will be executed or sent to labor camps. They want to make it impossible for you to operate in this region."

Jack felt a cold knot form in the pit of his stomach. "When? And how do you know all this?"

"72 hours," Richter replied. "And I know because I helped plan it. Or rather, I was supposed to. It was my chance to prove my loyalty once and for all."

"Your loyalty?" Jack couldn't keep the skepticism from his voice. "To which side, exactly?"

Richter's eyes hardened. "To humanity, Captain. To what's right. I may wear this uniform, but I am not a Nazi. Not anymore."

Before Jack could respond, a commotion outside the door drew his attention. Tom burst in, his face a mask of urgency.

"Jack, we've got a problem. A big one."

"What now?" Jack asked, already rising to his feet.

"It's Eduard," Tom said, his voice tight. "He's gone. And he took our main radio with him."

Jack felt as if the floor had dropped out from under him. Eduard – Marianne's father, their link to the broader Resistance network – gone? And with their primary means of long-range communication?

"Lock down the entire compound," Jack ordered, his mind racing. "No one in or out. And get Henri in here. We need to—"

He was cut off by a harsh laugh from Richter. "So, the mole reveals himself at last. I wondered how long it would take."

Jack whirled on him. "What do you know about this?"

Richter's expression was grim. "Eduard Dupont has been feeding information to Oberst Wilhelm Müller for months. Probably longer. I suspected, but I couldn't prove it. Until now."

The revelation hit Jack like a physical blow. Eduard – a traitor? It seemed impossible. And yet... it would explain so much. The suspiciously accurate German counterstrikes, the close calls that had become increasingly frequent.

"Why?" Jack demanded. "Why would he betray his own daughter, his own cause?"

Richter shook his head. "That, I don't know. But Captain, you need to understand – Müller is not a man to be trifled with. He's brilliant, ruthless, and now he has your main line of communication. You need to warn your network, and fast."

Jack's mind was already shifting into tactical mode. "Tom, get every runner we have. I want messages sent to every Resistance cell within 50 kilometers. Use the emergency codes. Tell them to go dark, change all their protocols. Eduard knows too much – we have to assume every safe house, every cache, every contact is compromised."

As Tom hurried off to carry out his orders, Jack turned back to Richter. "You're coming with us. You know Müller, you know this operation. We're going to need every scrap of intel you can provide."

Richter nodded, then grimaced as he tried to sit up. "I'll tell you everything I know, Captain. But you should understand – this isn't just about the Resistance anymore. Müller's ambitions go far beyond this little corner of France. If Operation Harvest Moon succeeds, it will be a model for pacifying occupied territories across Europe. Millions could die."

The enormity of what they were facing settled over Jack like a shroud. He'd known the stakes were high, but this... this was beyond anything he'd imagined.

"Alright," he said, helping Richter to his feet. "Let's get you to the command center. We've got a lot of work to do and precious little time to do it."

As they made their way through the underground complex, Jack's mind was racing. The loss of Eduard and the radio was a crippling blow, but they couldn't afford to dwell on it. They needed to adapt, to find new ways to communicate and coordinate their scattered forces.

In the command center, they found Henri and several other Resistance leaders gathered around a large map table. The atmosphere was tense, faces grim as they processed the news of Eduard's betrayal.

"Mes amis," Henri said as Jack and Richter entered. "The situation is grave. We've lost contact with three of our outlying cells. It seems Eduard has been busy."

Jack nodded, unsurprised but disheartened. "We need alternatives. Ways to get messages out that the Germans can't intercept."

One of the younger Resistance fighters – Pierre, Jack remembered – spoke up. "What about the old smuggling tunnels? The ones that run under half the villages in the region? We could use them to move runners between cells."

Henri stroked his mustache thoughtfully. "It could work. Many of those tunnels haven't been used in years. The Germans might not even know they exist."

"Do it," Jack ordered. "But be careful. We can't risk losing any more people."

As the group began to plan out routes and assign runners, Jack felt a presence at his elbow. He turned to find Marianne standing there, pale and unsteady but determined.

"You shouldn't be up," he said softly, concern evident in his voice.

Marianne shook her head. "I heard about my father. I... I need to help, Jack. I can't just lie there while everything falls apart."

Jack wanted to protest, to order her back to bed. But he knew that steely look in her eyes. There would be no dissuading her.

"Alright," he said. "But you stay here, in the command center. No field work. Understood?"

She nodded, relief evident on her face. "Thank you. Now, what can I do?"

For the next several hours, the command center was a hive of activity. Messages were drafted, coded, and sent out through every channel they could muster. Runners disappeared into the tunnel network, carrying vital intelligence to outlying cells. Every scrap of information Richter could provide about Operation Harvest Moon was analyzed, mapped, and factored into their evolving strategy.

As the sun began to set, casting long shadows through the narrow windows of their underground base, Jack found himself alone with Marianne for the first time since the chaos had begun.

"How are you holding up?" he asked gently, noting the lines of exhaustion etched on her face.

Marianne managed a wan smile. "I've been better. But I'll manage. It's just..." She trailed off, her eyes filling with tears she refused to let fall. "I can't believe my father would do this. After everything we've been through, everything we've fought for..."

Jack pulled her into a gentle embrace, mindful of her injuries. "I'm so sorry, Marianne. I can't imagine what you're going through."

She clung to him for a moment, allowing herself this brief vulnerability. Then, with visible effort, she straightened, wiping her eyes. "We can't dwell on it. There's too much at stake. Tell me, Jack – do you think we have a chance? Truly?"

Jack considered the question carefully. The odds were stacked against them, that much was certain. They were outgunned, outmanned, and now, thanks to Eduard's betrayal, potentially outmaneuvered as well. And yet...

"I think we do," he said finally. "It won't be easy. We'll have to be smarter, faster, and more creative than ever before. But if there's one thing I've learned about the people here, it's that they don't know how to give up. And neither do I."

Marianne nodded, her eyes blazing with determination. "Whatever it takes, Jack. We'll stop Operation Harvest Moon and make my father regret the day he turned traitor."

Jack squeezed her shoulder gently. "We will. But first, we need to focus on our immediate priorities."

He turned to the gathered team - Tom and Henri. "Alright, here's the plan. Tom, I want you and Henri to scout the German positions around the village. We need to know exactly what we're up against."

Tom nodded, already checking his gear. "Got it, boss. We'll be ghosts."

"Henri," Jack continued, "I need you on the radio. Monitor all frequencies, see if you can pick up any chatter about troop movements or Operation Harvest Moon."

"Oui, Captain," Henri replied, moving towards the battered radio set.

"Marianne," Jack said, turning back to her, "you know this area better than anyone. I need you to map out potential escape routes and safe houses. If things go south, we'll need options."

Marianne nodded, her face set with grim determination. "Consider it done."

As the group dispersed to their various tasks, Jack found himself alone with Henri. The old Resistance fighter regarded him with a knowing look.

"You carry a heavy burden, my friend," Henri said. "The weight of many lives rests on your shoulders."

Jack nodded, feeling the truth of those words in his very bones. "Sometimes I wonder if I'm the right man for this job," he admitted. "If I'm making the right choices."

Henri laid a gnarled hand on Jack's shoulder. "Doubt is the constant companion of a good leader," he said. "It is those who never question themselves that we should fear. You have earned the trust and respect of these people, Captain Holloway. Do not doubt that."

Jack felt a warmth spread through him at the old man's words. "Thank you, Henri. I just hope I can live up to that trust."

As he turned to go, to return to the endless tasks that awaited him, Jack's eye caught a small scrap of paper tacked to the wall. It was a quote, written in faded ink:

"Dans les moments de crise, seule l'imagination est plus importante que la connaissance." - Albert Einstein

"In times of crisis, imagination is more important than knowledge."

Jack allowed himself a small smile. Imagination. Perhaps that was the key. They couldn't match the Germans in firepower or numbers. But in creativity, in the ability to adapt and overcome... there, perhaps, lay their true strength.

With renewed determination, Jack strode back into the command center. They had a long night ahead, and dawn would bring new challenges. But for now, in this underground sanctuary, the spirit of resistance burned bright.

And as long as that flame endured, there was hope.

ᚦᚦᚦ

17
Firelight Confessions

❦

The old stone fireplace crackled and popped, casting flickering shadows across the worn faces gathered around it. Outside, the wind howled, carrying with it the first bitter chill of autumn. But here, in this hidden cellar beneath an abandoned farmhouse, a small group of resistance fighters found a moment of respite from the gathering storm.

Jack Holloway sat on an overturned crate, his elbows resting on his knees as he stared into the dancing flames. The events of the past few days weighed heavily on him – Eduard's betrayal, the looming threat of Operation Harvest Moon, the desperate scramble to reestablish their communication network. He felt stretched thin, like a wire about to snap.

A soft touch on his shoulder startled him from his brooding. He looked up to find Marianne standing beside him, two chipped mugs in her hands.

"Here," she said, offering him one. "It's not much, but it's hot."

Jack accepted the mug gratefully, inhaling the familiar scent of chicory coffee. "Thanks," he murmured, taking a sip. The bitter liquid burned its way down his throat, a welcome jolt to his weary system.

Marianne settled beside him, wincing slightly as the movement pulled at her healing wound. For a moment, they sat in companionable silence, each lost in their own thoughts.

It was Henri who finally broke the quiet. The old resistance fighter cleared his throat, drawing everyone's attention. "My friends," he began, his voice gravelly with age and too many cigarettes, "I think perhaps it is time we shared our burdens. We face dark days ahead, and secrets... secrets have a way of festering, of turning allies against each other."

Jack felt a ripple of tension go through the group. They all had their secrets, their hidden fears and regrets. But Henri was right – if they were going to survive what was coming, they needed to trust each other completely.

"I'll start, shall I?" Henri said, a sad smile playing at the corners of his mouth. He took a long drag on his cigarette, then began to speak. "You all know me as a resistance fighter, a leader in our cause. But there was a time, long ago, when I wore a different uniform."

A murmur went through the group. Jack leaned forward, intrigued despite himself.

"It was the Great War," Henri continued. "I was young, foolish, filled with dreams of glory. I fought for France, yes, but I also fought for myself. For recognition, for medals, for a chance to prove my worth." He paused, his eyes distant with memory. "I got my wish. I became a hero, decorated for valor. But the cost..." He shook his head. "The things I did, the lives I took... they haunt me still."

The old man's words hung heavy in the air. Jack found himself wondering how many other veterans of that long-ago conflict were now fighting this new war, carrying the weight of old sins along with their current burdens.

"Thank you for sharing that, Henri," Marianne said softly. She took a deep breath, then continued. "I suppose... I suppose it's my turn."

Jack turned to her, seeing the conflict playing out across her face. He wanted to reach out, to offer comfort, but he held back, sensing she needed to do this on her own.

"You all know about my father's betrayal," Marianne began, her voice barely above a whisper. "What you don't know is... I suspected. For weeks now, I've had this feeling, this nagging doubt. Little things that didn't add up, conversations that felt... off." She closed her eyes, a single tear tracing its way down her cheek. "I should have said something. Should have trusted my instincts. But I couldn't... couldn't bring myself to believe it. And now..."

"It's not your fault," Jack said firmly, unable to stay silent any longer. "Eduard made his choices. You can't blame yourself for his actions."

Marianne gave him a grateful look, but he could see the guilt still lingering in her eyes. "Perhaps," she said. "But I will carry this weight for a long time, I think."

The confessions continued, each member of the group sharing some hidden part of themselves. Tom spoke of the brother he'd left behind in America, of the guilt he felt for choosing to fight in a foreign war while his family struggled. The young radio operator, Simone, revealed that she'd been engaged to a German soldier before the occupation, and the conflict that still raged in her heart.

Through it all, Jack listened, feeling a growing sense of connection to these people who had become more than comrades – they were family now, bound by shared struggle and sacrifice.

Finally, all eyes turned to him. Jack felt the weight of their expectation, the silent question hanging in the air. He took a deep breath, steeling himself for what he was about to share.

"I've never told anyone this," he began, his voice low. "Not even my commanding officers back in London." He paused, gathering his thoughts. "Before I joined the OSS, before I became Captain Jack Holloway... I was someone else. Someone with a different name, a different life."

The room fell silent, all attention focused on Jack's words.

"I was born Jacob Heller," he continued. "Son of German immigrants in New York. When the war broke out, I... I changed my name. Enlisted under a false identity. I was afraid, you see. Afraid of being seen as the enemy, of being mistrusted because of my heritage."

He looked up, meeting the eyes of each person in the room. "I've spent this entire war hiding a part of myself, ashamed of where I came from. But being here, fighting alongside all of you... it's made me realize something. It's not where we come from that defines us. It's the choices we make, the things we're willing to fight for."

For a long moment, no one spoke. Then Marianne reached out, taking Jack's hand in hers. "Thank you for trusting us with this," she said softly. "It can't have been easy to carry that secret for so long."

Jack felt a weight lift from his shoulders, one he hadn't even realized he'd been carrying. "No," he agreed. "It wasn't. But it feels... it feels good to finally say it out loud."

Henri raised his mug in a toast. "To honesty," he said. "And to the family we choose."

The others echoed the sentiment, a newfound warmth and understanding flowing through the group. As they drank, Jack caught Richter's eye across the fire. The former SS officer had remained silent throughout the confessions, his face an unreadable mask.

"What about you, Richter?" Jack asked, unable to keep a challenging note from his voice. "Any secrets you'd like to share?"

Richter considered for a moment, then nodded slowly. "Very well," he said. "You've all been honest. I suppose I owe you the same courtesy."

He leaned forward, the firelight casting deep shadows across his face. "You know I was SS. What you don't know is why I joined in the first place." He paused, his expression distant. "I believed in it. Truly, deeply believed. The rhetoric, the promises of a greater Germany... I swallowed it all."

A ripple of tension went through the group at this admission. Richter held up a hand, forestalling any interruptions. "Let me finish," he said. "I believed... until I saw the reality of what we were doing. The camps. The executions. The systematic destruction of everything I thought we stood for."

His voice grew softer, filled with a pain that seemed to come from the depths of his soul. "I've done terrible things. Things I can never atone for, no matter how many lives I save now. But I swear to you all, on everything I hold sacred – I am no longer that man. I will fight with every breath in my body to stop what is coming, to undo some small part of the evil I once supported."

Silence fell over the group as they processed Richter's words. Jack studied the man's face, looking for any sign of deception. But all he saw was raw, honest pain and a desperate need for redemption.

Finally, Henri spoke. "It takes great courage to admit such things," he said gravely. "Especially to those who have every reason to hate you. I cannot speak for the others, but for my part... I believe you, Herr Richter. And I am glad to have you fighting at our side."

Murmurs of agreement rippled through the group. Jack felt a shift in the atmosphere, a sense of barriers falling away. They were no longer just a collection of individuals united by a common cause. They were becoming something more – a true team, bound by shared vulnerability and trust.

As the night wore on, the conversation turned to lighter topics. Old jokes were shared, stories of close calls and narrow escapes. Laughter, so rare in these dark times, filled the cellar. Jack found himself relaxing for the first time in what felt like years, allowing himself to simply be present in this moment of warmth and camaraderie.

It was well past midnight when the group finally began to disperse, each heading to their assigned sleeping spots. Jack lingered by the dying fire, not quite ready to face the solitude of his own thoughts.

He sensed rather than heard Marianne's approach. She settled beside him, close enough that he could feel the warmth of her body.

"Penny for your thoughts, Captain?" she asked softly.

Jack smiled, turning to face her. In the fading firelight, her eyes seemed to glow with an inner fire. "Just thinking about how strange life is," he said. "A few months ago, I was in London, planning operations from the safety of an office. Now here I am, in the heart of occupied France, sitting by a fire with the most remarkable group of people I've ever met."

Marianne's lips curved in a gentle smile. "Do you regret it? Coming here?"

Jack shook his head without hesitation. "Not for a second. Despite everything – the danger, the losses, the uncertainty – I've never felt more alive. More... purposeful."

He paused, gathering his courage for what he wanted to say next. "And I've never felt more connected to anyone than I do to you, Marianne."

Her breath caught, her eyes widening slightly. "Jack..." she began, but he pressed on, needing to get the words out.

"I know this isn't the time or place for... for whatever this is between us. We're in the middle of a war, facing impossible odds. But I need you to know – whatever happens in the days ahead, you've changed me. Made me a better man, a better leader. And if we survive this..."

Marianne silenced him with a finger to his lips. "No 'ifs,'" she said firmly. "We will survive this, Jack. We'll stop Operation Harvest Moon, we'll drive the Nazis from France, and then..." She leaned in, her lips barely brushing his. "Then we'll have all the time in the world to explore whatever this is between us."

Jack's heart raced as he closed the distance between them, kissing her with all the pent-up emotion of the past months. It was a promise, a declaration, a moment of perfect connection in the midst of chaos.

When they finally parted, both slightly breathless, Jack rested his forehead against hers. "I'll hold you to that," he murmured.

Marianne's answering smile was radiant. "I'm counting on it, mon capitaine."

As they sat there, wrapped in each other's arms by the dying embers of the fire, Jack felt a renewed sense of purpose flood through him. They had a long, hard road ahead. Operation Harvest Moon still loomed, a shadow over all their plans. Eduard's betrayal had left wounds that would take time to heal.

But in this moment, with Marianne by his side and the memory of tonight's shared confessions warming his heart, Jack knew one thing with absolute certainty – they would face whatever came next together. And somehow, that made all the difference in the world.

The fire guttered and went out, plunging the cellar into darkness. But Jack felt no fear. For in that darkness, he had found a light that would guide him through the trials to come.

Tomorrow would bring new challenges, new dangers. But for now, in this stolen moment of peace, Jack allowed himself to hope. To dream of a future beyond the war, beyond the pain and sacrifice. A future with Marianne, with the family they had forged in the crucible of resistance.

As sleep finally claimed him, Jack's last conscious thought was a silent vow – to fight with everything he had to make that future a reality. For Marianne. For his team. For the millions counting on them to succeed.

The fire may have gone out, but the flame of resistance burned brighter than ever in his heart.

ppp

18

Dawn Patrol

Mist at pre-dawn clung to the French countryside like a shroud, muffling sound and obscuring vision. Jack Holloway crouched at the edge of a farmer's field, his eyes straining to penetrate the gloom. Beside him, Marianne Dupont lay still as a statue, her steady breathing the only sign she was alive.

They had been in position for hours, waiting for the German patrol they knew would pass by. It was a calculated risk – getting this close to enemy forces could easily end in disaster. But they needed information, concrete details about the troop movements that heralded the start of Operation Harvest Moon.

Jack glanced at Marianne, marveling not for the first time at her composure. The betrayal of her father still weighed heavily on her, he knew. But she had channeled her pain and anger into a laser-like focus on their mission. In the days since their fireside confessions, he had seen a new steel in her eyes, a determination that both inspired and worried him.

A faint rumble in the distance caught his attention. He tensed, feeling Marianne do the same beside him. Slowly, cautiously, she raised her binoculars to her eyes.

"Two trucks," she whispered, her voice barely audible. "Heavy canvas coverings. Could be troop transport, or supplies."

Jack nodded, his mind racing. If they could somehow get a look inside those trucks, it could provide crucial intelligence about the German plans. But the risk...

Before he could voice his thoughts, Marianne was already moving. With a grace that belied her recent injury, she slipped from their hiding place and began making her way towards the road.

"Marianne!" Jack hissed, torn between admiration and frustration. "Wait!"

But she was already too far ahead. Cursing under his breath, Jack followed, keeping low and praying the mist would hold.

They reached the edge of the road just as the trucks came into view. Jack's heart pounded in his chest as he watched Marianne inch closer to the verge. What was she planning?

The answer came a moment later as she produced a small object from her pocket – a caltrops, a crude but effective tire-puncturing device. With a flick of her wrist, she sent it spinning onto the road, directly in the path of the lead truck.

The effect was instantaneous. There was a loud pop, followed by the screech of brakes and the angry shouts of German soldiers. The convoy ground to a halt, men spilling out of the trucks to assess the damage.

In the chaos that followed, Marianne darted forward, using the confusion to her advantage. Jack watched in disbelief as she slipped around the back of the second truck, deftly cutting a small slit in the canvas cover and peering inside.

It was over in seconds. Before any of the Germans could spot her, Marianne was back at Jack's side, her eyes shining with a mixture of triumph and adrenaline.

"We need to go," she breathed. "Now."

They retreated into the mist, moving as quickly as stealth would allow. It wasn't until they were safely back in the cover of a dense copse that Jack allowed himself to relax slightly.

"That," he said, fixing Marianne with a stern look, "was incredibly reckless."

She met his gaze unflinchingly. "It was necessary. And it paid off." She pulled a folded piece of paper from her jacket. "I managed to snag this from inside the truck. It looks like deployment orders, Jack. Details about troop movements, supply lines..."

Jack's annoyance faded as he realized the importance of what she had accomplished. "Marianne, this... this could be the break we've been looking for."

She nodded, a grim smile playing at her lips. "It's not everything, but it's a start. We can use this to start piecing together the full scope of Operation Harvest Moon."

As the adrenaline of their close call began to fade, Jack found himself studying Marianne's face in the soft morning light. There was a new intensity there, a fire that both thrilled and worried him.

"Marianne," he said softly, reaching out to brush a strand of hair from her face. "I know you're determined to stop this operation, to make things right after what your father did. But you can't... we can't afford to take unnecessary risks. I can't lose you."

Something flickered in her eyes – a softening, a moment of vulnerability. "Jack," she began, but he pressed on.

"I mean it. What we're doing here, it's bigger than any one of us. But that doesn't mean our lives are expendable. Promise me you'll be more careful."

Marianne was silent for a long moment. Then, slowly, she nodded. "I promise," she said quietly. "But Jack, you have to understand. This fight... it's all I have left. My home, my family, my whole world has been torn apart by this war. If I can play a part in ending it, in driving the Nazis from France... I have to do whatever it takes."

Jack felt a complex swirl of emotions – admiration, fear, and a love so fierce it almost took his breath away. He pulled Marianne close, feeling her relax into his embrace.

"I know," he murmured into her hair. "And I love you for it. But remember, you're not alone in this fight. We're in it together. All of us."

Marianne pulled back slightly, meeting his gaze. "Together," she agreed, a small smile touching her lips. Then, with a hint of her old mischief, she added, "Though I have to say, Captain, your idea of a romantic morning stroll leaves something to be desired."

Jack chuckled, grateful for the moment of levity. "Next time I'll try for a nice picnic by the Seine. How's that sound?"

"It's a date," Marianne said, her smile widening. Then, more seriously, "But first, we have a war to win."

With a nod, Jack straightened, his mind already turning to their next move. "Right. Let's get this intel back to base. Tom and Richter need to see this as soon as possible."

As they made their way back through the misty fields, Jack couldn't shake a sense of foreboding. They had scored a victory, yes, but at what cost? How many more close calls could they survive?

The Resistance safehouse was a hive of activity when they arrived. Tom met them at the door, his face a mask of tension.

"Thank God you're back," he said, ushering them inside. "We've got a situation."

Jack felt his stomach clench. "What kind of situation?"

Tom led them to the makeshift command center, where Richter and Henri were hunched over a map, their faces grim. "Our operatives in Paris just got word," Tom explained. "The Germans are moving up their timetable for Operation Harvest Moon. It's starting in 48 hours."

Jack felt the blood drain from his face. "48 hours? That's not possible. We're nowhere near ready."

Richter looked up, his expression grave. "It gets worse. They're bringing in additional SS units from the Eastern Front. Hardened veterans with experience in... pacification operations."

The implications hung heavy in the air. These weren't just ordinary soldiers. They were men accustomed to brutality, to the systematic destruction of entire communities.

"We have to warn the villages," Marianne said, her voice tight with urgency. "Get as many people to safety as we can."

Henri nodded. "I've already sent runners to our outlying cells. But Jack..." He hesitated, looking older and more tired than Jack had ever seen him. "Even if we evacuate every village in the region, it won't be enough. The Germans will just keep pushing, keep destroying until there's nothing left."

Jack felt the weight of command settle heavily on his shoulders. They all looked to him now, waiting for a plan, for some miracle that would save them from the coming storm.

He took a deep breath, centering himself. "Alright," he said, his voice steadier than he felt. "We knew this was coming. Now we just have to accelerate our own plans. Marianne, show them what we found."

As Marianne spread out the captured deployment orders, Jack began to pace, his mind racing. "Tom, I need you to get on the radio to London. Tell them what's happening, see if they can expedite any support they were planning to send. Air drops, sabotage teams, anything."

Tom nodded, already moving towards the communications room. Jack turned to Richter. "You know these SS units, their tactics. I need you to work with Henri, come up with strategies to counter them. Focus on delaying actions, ambushes, anything that can slow them down and buy us time."

"And what about you, Captain?" Henri asked. "What will you be doing?"

Jack's expression hardened. "I'm going to find my father-in-law."

A shocked silence fell over the room. Marianne was the first to recover. "Jack, what are you talking about? My father... he's gone. He betrayed us."

"Exactly," Jack said, turning to face her. "He betrayed us, which means he has information the Germans want. Information about our operations, our safe houses, our entire network. If Operation Harvest Moon is starting early, it's a good bet Eduard had something to do with it."

Richter nodded slowly, understanding dawning on his face. "You think if we can find Eduard, we can disrupt the German plans. Maybe even feed them false information."

"It's a long shot," Jack admitted. "But right now, it might be our best chance at throwing a wrench in their operation."

Marianne stepped forward, her eyes blazing. "I'm coming with you."

Jack opened his mouth to protest, but the look on her face stopped him. This wasn't just about the mission for her. This was personal. She needed closure, needed to confront her father and understand why he had betrayed everything they had fought for.

"Alright," he said softly. "We'll do this together."

As the others dispersed to carry out their assigned tasks, Jack pulled Marianne aside. "Are you sure about this?" he asked. "Facing your father... it won't be easy."

Marianne's expression was a mixture of pain and determination. "No, it won't be. But it's necessary. Not just for the mission, but for me. I need to know why, Jack. I need to look him in the eye and understand how he could do this to us. To France."

Jack nodded, understanding all too well the need for answers. He pulled her close, pressing a gentle kiss to her forehead. "Whatever happens," he murmured, "whatever we find out, just remember – you're not alone. I'm here. Always."

Marianne leaned into him, drawing strength from his presence. "I know," she said softly. "And that's what gives me the courage to face this."

As they broke apart, Jack saw a flicker of something in Marianne's eyes – a mix of love, fear, and a steely resolve that took his breath away. In that moment, he knew with absolute certainty that he would follow this woman anywhere, face any danger at her side.

The next few hours passed in a blur of preparation. Maps were studied, weapons cleaned and checked, contingency plans made and discarded. Through it all, Jack felt a growing sense of urgency, a knowledge that they were racing against time itself.

As night fell, Jack found himself standing outside the safehouse, staring up at the star-filled sky. How many more nights like this would there be, he wondered. How many more moments of quiet before the storm broke?

He sensed rather than heard Marianne's approach. She slipped her hand into his, a gesture of comfort and solidarity.

"Are you ready for this?" she asked softly.

Jack squeezed her hand gently. "As ready as I'll ever be. You?"

Marianne was silent for a long moment. When she spoke, her voice was barely above a whisper. "I'm scared, Jack. Not of the danger, not of what the Germans might do to us if we're caught. I'm scared of what I might do when I see my father. Of what I might become in that moment."

Jack turned to face her, cupping her face in his hands. "Listen to me," he said intently. "You are the strongest, bravest, most compassionate person I know. Whatever happens when we find Eduard, whatever you feel in that moment, it won't change who you are at your core. I believe in you, Marianne. Completely and without reservation."

Tears glistened in Marianne's eyes, but she blinked them back, a small smile touching her lips. "What did I do to deserve you, Jack Holloway?"

"I ask myself the same thing every day," he replied, leaning in to kiss her softly.

As they stood there, wrapped in each other's arms under the vast canopy of stars, Jack felt a surge of determination. They would find Eduard. They would stop Operation Harvest Moon. And somehow, someway, they would build a future together in a free France.

The odds were stacked against them, he knew. The coming days would test them in ways they couldn't even imagine. But in this moment, with Marianne by his side and the quiet strength of their team behind them, Jack allowed himself to hope.

Tomorrow, they would set out on their most dangerous mission yet. But tonight... tonight they had this moment of peace, this small pocket of warmth in a world gone cold with war.

As they finally turned to go back inside, Jack cast one last look at the star-filled sky. A shooting star blazed across the heavens, bright and fleeting.

Make a wish, his mother used to say on nights like this.

Jack closed his eyes briefly, sending a silent prayer into the vastness of the universe. Not for himself, not even for victory. But for Marianne, for their team, for all those who fought and suffered in this terrible war.

Let them find peace, he thought. Let them know a world without fear, without hatred. Let them live to see a dawn untroubled by the shadow of tyranny.

It was a fool's hope, perhaps. But as he followed Marianne back into the warmth of the safehouse, Jack clung to it like a lifeline. For in the dark days to come, hope might be the only thing that would see them through.

ᗐᗐᗐ

19

Race Against Time

The old Citroën groaned in protest as Jack guided it along the rutted country road. Dawn was just beginning to break, painting the sky in hues of pink and gold. Beside him, Marianne sat in tense silence, her eyes scanning the passing landscape for any sign of German patrols.

They had left the safehouse hours ago, armed with little more than a vague lead on Eduard's whereabouts and a desperate hope that they could somehow derail Operation Harvest Moon before it began. In the back seat, Tom fiddled with a portable radio, trying to pick up any German transmissions that might give them an edge.

"Anything?" Jack asked, glancing in the rearview mirror.

Tom shook his head, frustration evident on his face. "Nothing concrete. Lots of chatter about troop movements, but it's all in code. Without the cipher, it's useless to us."

Jack nodded grimly, returning his attention to the road. They were heading towards a small village called Montfort-sur-Lisle, where one of Henri's contacts had reported seeing a man matching Eduard's description. It was a long shot, but it was all they had.

As they crested a hill, the village came into view in the valley below. Jack felt Marianne tense beside him.

"This is it," she said softly. "This is where my father and I used to come every summer when I was a child. There's an old monastery just outside the village... he always loved the peace he found there."

Jack reached over, squeezing her hand gently. "It's a good place to start looking, then. You okay with this?"

Marianne nodded, her jaw set with determination. "I have to be. We need answers, and my father... he has to face the consequences of what he's done."

They parked the car on the outskirts of the village, not wanting to draw attention to themselves. As they made their way through the quiet streets, Jack was struck by how normal everything seemed. Shopkeepers were opening their stores, old men sat outside the local café sipping their morning coffee. It was hard to believe that in less than 48 hours, this peaceful scene could be shattered by the brutal efficiency of Operation Harvest Moon.

The monastery loomed before them, its ancient stone walls a testament to centuries of turbulent French history. As they approached the main gate, Jack felt a prickle of unease. It was too quiet. No birds singing, no sounds of life from within the walls.

"Something's wrong," he murmured, his hand going to the pistol concealed beneath his jacket.

Before Marianne or Tom could respond, the gate swung open. A figure stepped out – tall, distinguished, with silver hair and familiar eyes that widened in shock as they fell upon Marianne.

"Papa," Marianne breathed, her voice a mixture of pain and disbelief.

Eduard Dupont stood frozen for a moment, looking as if he'd seen a ghost. Then, to Jack's amazement, he began to run.

"Stop him!" Jack shouted, already sprinting after the older man.

They chased Eduard through the monastery grounds, past startled monks and through overgrown gardens. Despite his age, Eduard was surprisingly spry, leading them on a twisting path that seemed designed to confuse and misdirect.

Finally, they cornered him in a small courtyard. Eduard stood with his back to a stone wall, his chest heaving as he looked from Jack to Marianne to Tom.

"It's over, Monsieur Dupont," Jack said, keeping his voice level. "We need to talk."

Eduard's eyes darted around, looking for an escape route. Finding none, he slumped in defeat. "Very well," he said, his voice rough with emotion. "I suppose it was only a matter of time."

Marianne stepped forward, her face a mask of conflicting emotions. "Why, Papa?" she asked, her voice barely above a whisper. "How could you betray everything we fought for? Everything Maman died for?"

Eduard flinched as if he'd been struck. "You don't understand, ma chérie. None of you do. What I did... it was to protect you. To protect all of us."

Jack's eyes narrowed. "Protect us? By collaborating with the Nazis? By giving them information that will lead to the deaths of countless innocent people?"

"You think it's so simple?" Eduard snapped, a flash of anger breaking through his defeated demeanor. "You think I had a choice? They came to me, told me what they would do to Marianne, to our entire village if I didn't cooperate.

I thought... I thought I could play both sides, feed them just enough information to keep them satisfied while still helping the Resistance."

Marianne shook her head, tears streaming down her face. "But Papa, don't you see? Whatever your intentions, people have died because of the information you gave them. Our friends, our neighbors... their blood is on your hands."

Eduard seemed to age years before their eyes, the weight of his actions finally crashing down upon him. "I know," he said softly. "God help me, I know. And I will carry that guilt for the rest of my life. But Marianne, you have to believe me – everything I did, I did for you. To give you a chance at a future in a world gone mad."

Jack stepped forward, his voice hard. "That future is at risk now, Monsieur Dupont. The Germans are accelerating their plans. Operation Harvest Moon begins in less than two days. We need to know everything you told them, every detail about our operations, our safe houses, our contacts. It's the only way we have a chance of stopping this."

Eduard looked at him for a long moment, then nodded slowly. "Very well. I will tell you everything. But not here. It isn't safe."

As if to punctuate his words, the distant sound of engines reached their ears. Jack tensed, recognizing the distinctive rumble of German transport trucks.

"We need to move," Tom said urgently. "Now."

They made their way quickly back through the monastery, Eduard leading them to a hidden door that opened onto a narrow path winding into the surrounding woods. As they slipped away, Jack caught a glimpse of German soldiers pouring into the monastery grounds. They had escaped just in time.

For hours, they trekked through the dense forest, Eduard guiding them along hidden trails and long-forgotten smugglers' routes. As they walked, he began to talk, pouring out a tale of coercion, fear, and desperate attempts to mitigate the damage of his collaboration.

As they paused to catch their breath in a small glade, Jack decided it was time to press Eduard for more specific information.

"Monsieur Dupont," Jack began, his voice low but intense, "what exactly is Operation Harvest Moon? What are the Germans planning?"

Eduard's face clouded, a mix of fear and confusion crossing his features. "I... I'm not entirely sure," he admitted. "Most of it was kept from me. But I overheard things, saw glimpses..."

"What kind of glimpses?" Marianne urged, her hand finding her father's arm.

Eduard's eyes took on a distant look. "There was a room in the château... a laboratory of some kind. I saw men working there, always in white uniforms. Scientists, I think. They wouldn't let anyone in except for Sturmbannführer Müller."

"A lab?" Jack's brow furrowed. "Did you ever see what was inside?"

"No," Eduard shook his head. "But whatever it is, it's not good. I heard Müller talking about it once. He said it would 'bring France to its knees.' That it would 'destroy the very soul of the country.'"

A chill ran down Jack's spine. He exchanged a worried glance with Marianne.

They fell into an uneasy silence, each contemplating the ominous implications of Eduard's words. Whatever Operation Harvest Moon was, they knew they had to stop it.

The fate of France might depend on it.

"We need to keep moving," Jack said finally. "Whatever the Nazis are planning, we're running out of time to stop it."

With renewed urgency, they pressed on through the darkening forest, the mystery of the men in white uniforms and the secret laboratory weighing heavily on their minds.

As the sun began to set, they reached a small clearing. In the center stood a dilapidated hunting cabin, barely more than four walls and a roof.

"We'll be safe here for the night," Eduard said, pushing open the creaking door. "No one knows about this place except me."

Inside, they found basic supplies – canned food, water, even a few threadbare blankets. As Tom set about trying to establish radio contact with their base, Jack pulled Marianne aside.

"How are you holding up?" he asked softly, concern evident in his eyes.

Marianne managed a wan smile. "I'm... I don't know, Jack. Part of me wants to hate him for what he's done. But another part... I can see how much he's suffered, how the guilt is eating him alive. I don't know if I can forgive him, but I think I'm starting to understand."

Jack nodded, pulling her into a gentle embrace. "You're stronger than anyone I've ever known, Marianne. Whatever you decide, whatever happens next, I'm here for you. Always."

They stood like that for a long moment, drawing strength from each other. Then Tom's excited voice broke the silence.

"I've got them!" he called. "Base camp, coming in clear."

They gathered around the radio as Tom relayed their situation and the information they'd gathered from Eduard.

The response was swift and decisive.

"Change of plans," came Henri's voice, crackling with static. "We're mobilizing everything we have. Every Resistance cell in the region is going on the offensive. Hit-and-run attacks, sabotage, anything to disrupt the German preparations for Operation Harvest Moon. But we need more than that. We need a decisive blow."

Jack leaned in close to the radio. "What did you have in mind?"

"The intelligence you've gathered suggests that the operational headquarters for Harvest Moon is located in an old château near Giverny. If we can take it out, destroy their command and control capabilities, we might just be able to throw the entire operation into chaos."

Jack felt a surge of adrenaline at the audacity of the plan. It was risky, borderline suicidal even. But if it worked...

"We'll do it," he said firmly. "Give us the coordinates. We'll rendezvous with whatever forces you can spare and hit them with everything we've got."

As Tom jotted down the details, Jack turned to Eduard. "This is your chance," he said, his voice low and intense. "A chance to make things right. Will you help us?"

Eduard straightened, a flicker of his old fire returning to his eyes. "Yes," he said simply. "Whatever it takes."

They spent the next few hours planning, poring over maps and discussing tactics. Eduard's knowledge of German protocols and procedures proved invaluable as they formulated their assault plan.

As the others finally settled down to grab what sleep they could, Jack found himself unable to rest. He stepped outside, breathing in the cool night air. The weight of what they were about to attempt pressed down on him, a nearly physical force.

He sensed rather than heard Marianne's approach. She slipped her hand into his, a gesture that had become as natural as breathing.

"Second thoughts?" she asked softly.

Jack shook his head. "No. Just... thinking about what's at stake. If we fail..."

"We won't," Marianne said with quiet conviction. "We can't. Too many people are counting on us."

Jack turned to face her, struck once again by the strength and beauty of this remarkable woman. "Marianne," he began, his voice thick with emotion. "When this is over, when we've stopped Operation Harvest Moon and driven the Nazis from France... marry me."

Marianne's eyes widened in surprise at Jack's proposal, then softened with a love so intense it took his breath away. "Yes," she whispered, her voice trembling with emotion. "A thousand times, yes."

They came together slowly, as if drawn by an irresistible force. Jack's hand gently cupped Marianne's face, his thumb brushing across her cheekbone. Marianne's fingers tangled in the fabric of Jack's shirt, pulling him closer.

Their lips met, and the world around them seemed to fade away. The kiss was tender at first, a gentle exploration filled with unspoken promises. Then, as if a dam had broken, it deepened into something more passionate, more urgent.

Jack's arms encircled Marianne's waist, drawing her flush against him. He could feel the rapid beating of her heart, matching the frantic rhythm of his own. Marianne's hands slid up to tangle in Jack's hair, holding him close as if afraid he might disappear if she let go.

The kiss seemed to last an eternity, a moment suspended in time. It was a declaration of love, a defiance against the darkness that surrounded them, a promise of a future they would fight with everything they had to secure.

When they finally parted, both were breathless. Jack rested his forehead against Marianne's, unwilling to put even the slightest distance between them. Their eyes met, and in that gaze was a world of emotion – love, hope, fear, and an unwavering determination to face whatever came next, together.

"Whatever happens tomorrow," Jack murmured, his voice husky with emotion, "know that loving you has been the greatest adventure of my life."

Marianne's answering smile was radiant, her eyes shining with unshed tears of joy. "And we're just getting started, mon amour," she whispered back. "We have a whole lifetime of adventures ahead of us."

They stood there, wrapped in each other's arms under a canopy of stars, savoring this moment of peace and connection amidst the chaos of war. In this kiss, they had found a shelter from the storm, a reminder of what they were fighting for, and the strength to face the challenges that lay ahead.

Dawn broke, painting the sky in shades of pink and gold. Jack and his team made their final preparations, checking weapons and going over the plan one last time. Eduard, looking more alive than he had in days, provided last-minute insights into German defenses and protocols.

As they prepared to leave the safety of the cabin, Jack gathered everyone around.

"I won't lie to you," he said, his voice steady and clear. "What we're about to do is incredibly dangerous. Some of us may not make it back. But what we do today could change the course of this war, could save countless lives. Remember that. Remember why we fight."

He met each of their eyes in turn, seeing the same mix of determination and fear that he felt in his own heart.

"Whatever happens," he continued, "I want you to know that it has been the greatest honor of my life to serve with you. You are not just my team – you are my family."

A moment of silence fell over the group, heavy with unspoken emotion. Then Tom stepped forward, extending his hand. "For France," he said simply.

One by one, the others joined in, their hands forming a circle of unity and resolve. "For freedom," Marianne added. "For justice," said Eduard. "For all those who can't fight for themselves," Jack finished.

As they broke apart, Jack felt a surge of pride and affection for this unlikely band of heroes. Whatever the outcome of the coming battle, he knew they would face it together, united in purpose and bound by a bond stronger than any forged in peacetime.

They moved out, making their way through the early morning mist towards the rendezvous point where they would meet up with the other Resistance fighters. The château that served as the German headquarters loomed in the distance, a dark silhouette against the brightening sky.

Jack felt Marianne's hand slip into his as they walked. No words were needed – in that simple gesture was a world of understanding, of shared purpose and unwavering love.

As they approached the gathering point, Jack saw faces both familiar and new – men and women from all walks of life, united by their determination to free their country from Nazi oppression. Henri was there, looking grim but resolute as he coordinated the final preparations.

Jack took a deep breath, squaring his shoulders as he prepared to address the assembled fighters. This was it – the moment that would determine the fate of countless lives, the future of France itself.

In the distance, the first sounds of gunfire could be heard – the opening salvos of the Resistance's coordinated attacks across the region. Operation Harvest Moon was beginning, but so too was the fight to stop it.

As the sun began to set, Jack gathered his team for one final briefing. The mood was tense, each person acutely aware that the coming hours would likely define not just their own fates, but that of countless others across occupied France.

"This is it," Jack said, his voice low but steady. "Everything we've fought for, everything we've lost – it all comes down to tonight. I won't lie to you; the odds are stacked against us. But I've seen what this team can do, what we're capable of when we work together."

He met each pair of eyes in turn – Tom's determined gaze, Henri's weathered but unwavering stare, Marianne's fierce, burning look. Even Eduard, seeking redemption for his past betrayal, stood tall and ready.

"Get some rest," Jack continued. "We move out at 0300 hours. And remember – whatever happens in that château, we're making history. For France. For freedom. For all those who can't fight for themselves."

As the others dispersed to make their final preparations, Marianne lingered. She approached Jack, her expression a complex mix of emotions.

"Jack," she said softly. "I need you to promise me something."

He turned to her, struck once again by her beauty, her strength. "Anything," he replied without hesitation.

Marianne took a deep breath. "Promise me that, no matter what happens in there, you'll see this through to the end. That you'll finish what we started, even if... even if I'm not there to see it."

Jack felt a chill run down his spine. "Marianne, don't talk like that. We're going to make it through this. Together."

She smiled, but it didn't quite reach her eyes. "Of course we are. But promise me anyway. Please."

He pulled her close, breathing in her familiar scent of lavender and gunpowder. "I promise," he whispered into her hair. "But you're not getting out of our future together that easily, you hear me?"

Marianne's laugh was soft and a little sad. "I wouldn't dream of it, mon capitaine."

As they parted, Jack couldn't shake a sense of foreboding. He pushed it aside, focusing instead on the mission ahead. In a few short hours, they would be assaulting the very heart of Nazi power in the region. The fate of Operation Harvest Moon – and perhaps the entire French Resistance – hung in the balance.

The night passed in a blur of last-minute preparations and tense silence. Sleep, when it came, was fitful and filled with disjointed dreams of battles past and yet to come. As the hour of their departure approached, Jack felt an eerie calm settle over him. Whatever happened in the coming hours, he knew there was no turning back.

As they neared their objective, Jack signaled for the group to halt. Ahead, barely visible in the fading night, loomed the imposing silhouette of the château. It was time.

ppp

20
The Storm Breaks

Jack Holloway surveyed the German headquarters from their hidden vantage point as the pre-dawn air hung thick with tension. The château loomed before them, its once-elegant facade now bristling with machine gun nests and searchlights. In the courtyard below, he could make out the shapes of tanks and troop transports, a grim reminder of the overwhelming force they were up against.

The hours since their final briefing had passed in a blur of last-minute preparations and tense silence. Now, as the moment of truth approached, Jack felt an eerie calm settle over him. Whatever happened in the coming hours, he knew there was no turning back.

Beside him, Marianne lay still as a statue, her eyes fixed on the building through a pair of binoculars. "I count at least thirty guards on the perimeter," she murmured. "Heavy weapons emplacements here, here, and here." She pointed out the positions on the crude map spread between them.

Jack nodded, his mind racing as he finalized their approach. They had one shot at this – one chance to disrupt Operation Harvest Moon before it could devastate the entire region. Failure wasn't an option.

He keyed his radio, his voice barely above a whisper. "All units, report in."

One by one, the responses came back. Tom and his team were in position to the east, ready to create a diversion that would draw attention away from their main assault. Henri and a group of local Resistance fighters were set up to the north, prepared to cut off any German reinforcements that might arrive. And Eduard... Jack still felt a twinge of unease at trusting Marianne's father, but the man's knowledge of German protocols had proven invaluable in planning their attack.

"Remember," Jack said, his voice steady despite the adrenaline coursing through his veins, "our primary objective is to reach the laboratory. If the intelligence is correct, that's where we'll find the heart of Operation Harvest Moon. Stick to the plan, watch each other's backs, and for God's sake, stay alive."

A chorus of affirmatives crackled over the radio. Jack took a deep breath, steeling himself for what was to come. He turned to Marianne, seeing his own mix of determination and fear mirrored in her eyes.

"Ready?" he asked softly.

Marianne nodded, a grim smile playing at the corners of her mouth. "Born ready, mon capitaine."

Jack allowed himself a moment to drink in the sight of her – fierce, beautiful, the woman he had come to care for deeply. Then he pushed the emotion aside, focusing on the task at hand.

"All units," he said into the radio, "Operation Firefly is a go. I say again, Firefly is a go."

For a heartbeat, nothing happened. Then the night erupted into chaos.

The eastern side of the château exploded in a ball of fire as Tom's team detonated their charges. Alarms blared, searchlights swung wildly, and the shouts of confused German soldiers filled the air.

"Move!" Jack ordered, and their assault team surged forward.

They raced across the open ground, using the confusion of the explosion to their advantage. Jack's heart pounded in his chest as bullets whizzed past, kicking up dirt at their feet. Beside him, Marianne moved with fluid grace, her Sten gun chattering as she provided covering fire.

They reached the château wall, pressing themselves against it as German machine guns opened up, raking the ground they had just crossed. Jack risked a glance around the corner, seeing a group of soldiers rushing towards their position.

"Grenade!" he shouted, pulling the pin and lobbing it around the corner. The explosion was followed by screams and a momentary lull in the gunfire.

"Now!" Jack yelled, and they burst into action once more.

The next few minutes were a blur of violence and adrenaline. They fought their way through the château's lower levels, every room a potential deathtrap. Jack moved on autopilot, years of training taking over as he cleared corners, took down enemies, and protected his team.

Marianne was a whirlwind beside him, her face set in a mask of grim determination as she fought with a ferocity that took his breath away. Together, they were unstoppable, anticipating each other's moves, covering each other's blind spots.

They reached the main staircase, only to find it heavily defended. German soldiers poured fire down from above, pinning them in place.

"We need to clear that stairwell!" Jack shouted over the din of battle.

Eduard appeared at his side, his face streaked with dirt and blood. "I have an idea," he said, pulling something from his pack. It was a bundle of grenades, wired together in a way Jack had never seen before.

"Where did you get that?" Jack demanded, even as he provided covering fire.

Eduard's smile was cold and humorless. "Let's just say I learned a few things during my time with our Nazi friends. Now, cover me!"

Before Jack could stop him, Eduard was moving, darting from cover to cover as he made his way towards the base of the stairs. German bullets rained down around him, but somehow, he made it.

With a yell of defiance, Eduard pulled a pin and hurled the improvised explosive up the stairwell. There was a moment of terrible silence, then a thunderous explosion that shook the entire château.

When the dust settled, the stairway was clear. But Eduard lay crumpled at its base, his body riddled with bullets.

"Papa!" Marianne's anguished cry cut through the ringing in Jack's ears. She started towards her fallen father, but Jack held her back.

"We have to keep moving," he said, hating himself for the words even as he spoke them. "We can't let his sacrifice be in vain."

Marianne's eyes blazed with a mixture of grief and rage, but she nodded. As they ascended the now-clear stairway, Jack saw her pause briefly beside Eduard's body, whispering something too soft for him to hear.

The upper levels of the château were a maze of corridors and rooms. They fought their way through, relying on the intelligence Eduard had provided to guide them towards the laboratory. The sounds of battle echoed from all around – it seemed the entire building had become a war zone.

Finally, they reached their objective. The door to the lab was heavily reinforced, designed to withstand attack.

"Plant the charges," Jack ordered, and his demolitions expert moved forward.

But before they could breach the door, a new sound cut through the chaos – the distinctive whine of Stuka dive bombers.

"They're calling in air support!" Tom shouted, his face pale with the realization of what that meant.

Jack's mind raced. If the Germans were willing to bomb their own headquarters, it meant they were desperate. It also meant that their mission was even more critical than they had realized.

"Change of plans," he said, his voice tight with urgency. "Tom, take half the team and set up anti-aircraft positions on the roof. Buy us as much time as you can. The rest of you, with me. We're going in."

The next few minutes were a blur of explosions, gunfire, and desperate hand-to-hand combat as they breached the laboratory. Jack fought with a cold fury, every German soldier he took down another step towards stopping the madness of Operation Harvest Moon.

Marianne was at his side through it all, her movements a deadly dance as she cleared the room with ruthless efficiency. In the back of his mind, Jack marveled at her strength, her ability to channel her grief into action.

As the last defender fell, they finally had a moment to take in their surroundings. The laboratory was a nightmare of gleaming equipment and mysterious chemical vats. At the center of it all stood a large industrial mixer, filled with a fine, grayish powder.

"My God," Jack breathed, realization dawning. "This is what Operation Harvest Moon is really about."

Marianne moved to a nearby workstation, rifling through papers. "It's a defoliant," she said, her voice tight with horror. "Designed to destroy vegetation on a massive scale. They're planning to spray it over our vineyards, our farms - everything."

Jack's mind reeled at the implications. "A scorched earth policy. They're going to try to destroy everything as they retreat."

"The devastation this could cause would be immeasurable," Marianne continued, "not just to our economy, but to the very soul of France."

Suddenly, a slow clap echoed through the laboratory. They whirled to see a tall, distinguished-looking German officer emerge from a hidden alcove.

"Bravo," he said, his voice dripping with sarcasm. "I must say, I'm impressed you made it this far. But I'm afraid your little raid ends here."

Jack raised his weapon, but the German was faster. In a lightning-quick move, he grabbed a nearby canister and hurled it towards them. It shattered at their feet, releasing a cloud of noxious gas.

Jack stumbled back, coughing violently. Through watering eyes, he saw Marianne crumple to the ground, clutching her face.

"Marianne!" he cried out, reaching for her even as his vision began to blur.

The German officer – Oberst Müller, Jack realized dimly – stepped forward, a gas mask protecting him from the fumes. "I wouldn't struggle if I were you," he said coldly. "The effects can be quite... unpleasant."

Jack fought against the encroaching darkness, but it was a losing battle. The last thing he saw before unconsciousness claimed him was Müller standing over Marianne's prone form, a look of cruel triumph on his face.

When Jack came to, he found himself bound to a chair in what looked like an opulent study. Marianne was beside him, similarly restrained. Her eyes were red and swollen from the gas, and Jack felt a stab of fear.

"Marianne," he whispered urgently. "Can you hear me? Are you alright?"

She stirred, turning her head towards his voice. "Jack? I... I can barely see. What happened?"

Before Jack could respond, the door opened and Müller strode in, flanked by two armed guards.

"Ah, our guests are awake," he said, smiling like a cat that had caught a particularly juicy mouse. "Excellent. We have much to discuss."

"You bastard," Jack snarled. "What have you done to her?"

Müller's smile didn't waver. "A regrettable necessity, I assure you. But perhaps a fitting one, given the blindness of your futile resistance." He paced before them, hands clasped behind his back. "You see, Operation Harvest Moon is far more than just a military campaign. It's about breaking the spirit of France itself."

He gestured towards a map on the wall, showing the agricultural regions of France. "Imagine it – every vineyard, every farm, every forest between here and Paris, reduced to ash and barren soil. Centuries of agricultural heritage, wiped out. The economic impact alone would be catastrophic. But more than that, it would strike at the very heart of French identity."

Jack felt a cold fury building inside him. "You're insane," he growled. "You'd destroy all that just to slow down the Allied advance?"

Müller's eyes hardened. "War requires sacrifices, Herr Holloway. We will leave France a wasteland as we withdraw. Your armies may advance, but they will find nothing but dust and ashes to sustain them."

As Müller monologued, Jack worked frantically at his bonds. He could feel them starting to give, just a little. If he could just buy some more time...

"You won't get away with this," Marianne said, her voice steady despite her injury. "The Resistance will stop you."

Müller laughed. "My dear, your little band of freedom fighters is finished. As we speak, my men are loading the first batches of our defoliant onto planes. Soon, the skies will rain destruction upon your precious homeland, and there will be nothing you can do to stop it."

Jack saw his chance. With a final, desperate effort, he broke free of his restraints and lunged at Müller. The German was caught off guard, and they went down in a tangle of limbs.

They grappled furiously, each fighting for control. Jack managed to get his hands around Müller's throat, but one of the guards intervened, slamming the butt of his rifle into Jack's back.

Jack rolled away, gasping in pain. He saw Müller scrambling for a pistol that had fallen during the scuffle. Time seemed to slow as Jack threw himself towards the weapon.

His hand closed around the grip just as Müller reached it. For a moment, they struggled for control. Then a shot rang out.

Müller's eyes widened in shock. He looked down to see a crimson stain spreading across his immaculate uniform. With a final, gurgling gasp, he collapsed.

Jack didn't have time to process what had happened. He spun, taking down the two guards with quick, precise shots. Then he was at Marianne's side, frantically working to free her.

"We have to move," he said urgently. "Can you see well enough to walk?"

Marianne nodded, her face pale but determined. "Just... just don't let go of me, okay?"

Jack's heart clenched at the vulnerability in her voice. "Never," he promised.

They made their way through the château, Jack guiding Marianne past obstacles and dispatching any German soldiers they encountered. The building shook with explosions – it seemed the air raid was in full swing.

As they neared the exit, Jack spotted a case labeled 'Chemical Analysis' in a nearby office. He grabbed it, praying it would contain information that could help them counteract the defoliant.

They burst out into the pre-dawn light just as the main tower collapsed behind them. Jack turned, watching as the once-proud building was reduced to rubble. Somewhere in there, beneath tons of stone and mortar, lay the body of Eduard Dupont and countless others who had given their lives for freedom.

As the dust settled, an eerie quiet fell over the battlefield. In the distance, Jack could hear the sound of retreating vehicles – the remnants of the German forces, fleeing in disarray.

"We did it," Tom said, appearing at Jack's side. His voice was filled with exhausted disbelief. "We actually did it."

Jack nodded, unable to speak past the lump in his throat. They had won, yes. Operation Harvest Moon was in ruins, the Nazi scorched earth plan dealt a significant blow. But the cost... God, the cost had been so high.

In the days that followed, Jack and the surviving members of the Resistance worked tirelessly. Using the chemical data they'd recovered and Marianne's brilliant mind – slowly recovering along with her eyesight – they managed to develop a method to neutralize the German defoliant.

As reports came in of farmlands and vineyards saved from destruction, Jack allowed himself a moment of bittersweet victory. They had preserved a crucial part of France's heritage and future economy. But the price had been steep. The scars of this battle, both physical and emotional, would take a long time to heal.

Standing amidst the rolling hills of the Dupont vineyard, Jack looked out over the land they had fought so hard to protect. Much had been lost, but much had been saved. And in that moment, watching the sun rise over the scarred but unbroken French countryside, he felt a flicker of hope for the future – for France, for Marianne, and for himself.

The war wasn't over. But they had won a critical battle. And whatever challenges lay ahead, Jack knew they would face them together, their resolve as enduring as the vines that had weathered this storm.

ᗐᗐᗐ

Epilogue

One week after the battle, Jack stood with Marianne in a small vineyard outside Saint-Clair-sur-Epte. The vines stood untouched, a testament to their success in halting Operation Harvest Moon. As he described the scene to Marianne, whose eyes were still recovering from the effects of the gas attack, familiar voices approached.

"Well, if it isn't the heroes of the hour! Thought you could save France without us, did you?"

Jack's heart leapt. "Mike? Cooper? Singh?"

Their old team approached, bearing the marks of recent ordeals but alive and ready for action. Mike, the explosives expert, sported a new scar. Cooper, their demolitions specialist, limped slightly. Singh, their taciturn radio operator, nodded silently.

"How?" Jack asked, emotion making his voice rough.

Cooper clapped Jack's shoulder. "Takes more than a few Nazis to keep us down, boss. We've been making our way back, gathering intel along the way."

Singh added softly, "We intercepted communications about Operation Harvest Moon. Came as fast as we could, but..." His eyes went to Marianne's healing face.

Marianne straightened her shoulders. "Don't you dare pity me," she said firmly. "We won. That's what matters."

Mike whistled low. "Damn, girl. Injured or not, you're still the toughest one here."

As they walked among the saved vines, Jack felt renewed purpose. The battle for France was far from over, but with his team reunited and Marianne by his side, hope felt tangible.

That night, as Jack and Marianne lay in the village inn, sleep proved elusive.

"Jack," Marianne whispered, "do you ever wonder if there's a point to all this suffering? If the world we're fighting for will truly be better?"

Jack considered her words. "I think the point isn't just about the world we're creating. It's about who we become in the process. This war has brought out the worst in humanity, yes. But it's also shown us the heights of courage and resilience we're capable of reaching."

Marianne nodded. "Like the villagers who risked everything to help us stop Operation Harvest Moon."

"Exactly," Jack agreed. "Maybe that's the real victory. Not just defeating the Nazis, but proving that even in the darkest times, there's still light in the human spirit."

Suddenly, a distant, unmistakable sound broke the pre-dawn quiet - the deep drone of heavy aircraft engines.

Jack was instantly alert, moving to the window. The sky was dark, but he could make out the silhouettes of planes overhead, far too many to be a German patrol.

Mike, Cooper, and Singh burst in, armed and ready.

"You hearing this?" Mike whispered.

Jack nodded grimly. "Yeah. A lot of aircraft."

Singh held up his radio. "I've been monitoring frequencies. Something big is happening, Jack."

The aircraft noise increased. The team tensed, weapons ready, prepared for anything.

But instead of bombs, papers fluttered down from the sky - leaflets by the thousands.

Jack snatched one out of the air, reading aloud: "People of France, the liberation has begun. Allied forces have landed in Normandy. The German occupiers are in retreat. Hold fast. Freedom is coming."

Singh's radio crackled, confirming the news: Allied forces advancing, German lines collapsing, Paris's liberation imminent.

Stunned silence fell over the group, then slowly, grins spread across their faces.

"It's really happening," Jack said, disbelief and joy mingling in his voice. "The tide's finally turning."

Marianne squeezed his hand, tears in her healing eyes. "Then we have work to do. This is just the beginning of the real fight."

Jack nodded. "Cooper, Singh - contact our local allies. We need to coordinate with the advancing forces. Mike, you're with me. Let's secure the village."

As they prepared to move out, Jack looked at each member of his team - his family. "Whatever comes next, we face it together."

They stepped out into the uncertain dawn, ready to play their part in France's liberation. More villagers emerged, drawn by the planes and leaflets. The atmosphere was electric, hope and apprehension mingling.

Jack described the scene to Marianne as they walked - faces lifted to the sky, leaflets carpeting the ground, Allied aircraft filling the air.

"You know," Jack said softly, "that future we fought for? The one where these vineyards thrive and our children play without fear?"

Marianne nodded, curious.

"I think we just took the first real step towards making it a reality," Jack continued. "Whatever happens next, whatever battles we still have to fight, I know we'll get there. Together."

Marianne squeezed his hand, her face radiant with hope. "Together," she agreed. "For France. For our future. For